# Dragonbound IV

# Red Dragon

## Rebecca Shelley

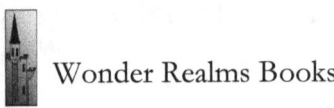 Wonder Realms Books

Cover art © Dusan Kostic | Dreamstime.com
Interior art © Rocich | Dreamstime.com


ISBN-13: 978-0615981437
ISBN-10: 0615981437

Published by Wonder Realms Books

For everyone who loves dragons.

# Dragonbound

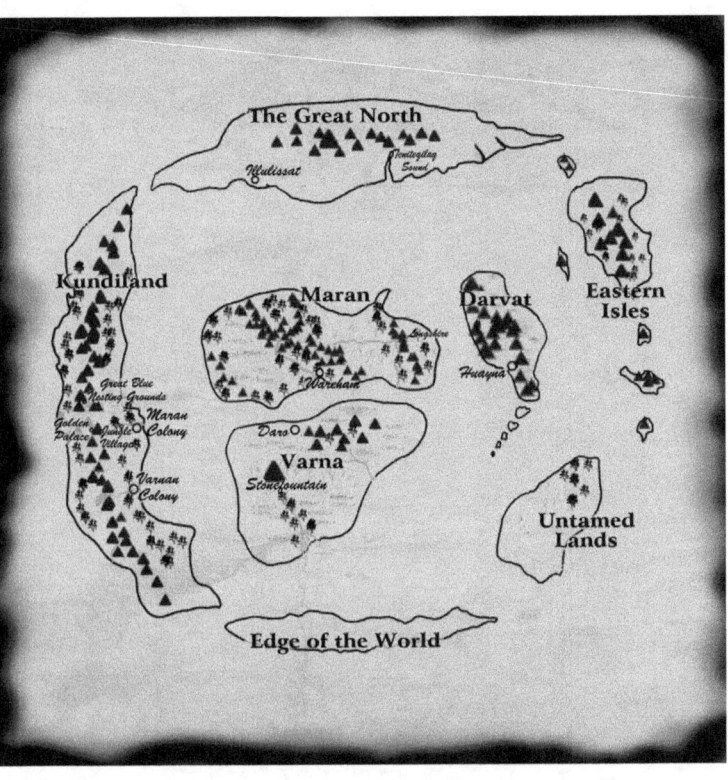

## Prologue

**The Naga finished his** dinner and climbed out of the pit. Blood and gore clung to the steel claws he wore over his hands. Claws for killing, tearing, and feasting. Claws to match his dragon claws. He shook himself. No construction could replace his wings. When he was in his dragon body, he could fly, but when his thoughts clung to this pitiful form, he was chained to the ground. He crawled hands and knees over the steaming black rock and scuttled into a tunnel that led to the great cavern. His dragon self was calling him back from the meal. His mind twisted with ferocious anticipation.

It was time. After waiting so long, it was time.

His dragon self emerged from the pool of magma at the center of the cavern, scales glowing red hot.

Sweat soaked the Naga, but the dragon knew better than to touch him so soon after basking in the lava. The pain was too intense. The Naga had plenty of scars from previous burns, but now his human self and his dragon self both understood they must stand away from each other until the dragon cooled and his scales crusted over with rough black rock.

*It is time,* his dragon self snarled. *The silver worm has returned from Maran. We must ready ourselves.*

The Naga prostrated himself on the rocks before his dragon self. *What must we do?*

*Get up. Stand on your back legs. You were human once. It is time to pretend to be human again.*

The Naga shuddered. He did not like to think of himself as one of the wretched humans that his dragon self kept in metal cages in the dark tunnels. He was not like them. Their minds were so feeble, so easy to twist and crush, so easy to control but so hard to keep alive. So hard to block their feelings from his own mind, to keep from being overcome by their pain and fear, sadness and desperate longing. He'd had to kill too many of them just to get them to stop crashing into his thoughts until he'd learned to build a shield around himself, learned how to force his sense of them back into the cages.

His dragon self growled. *Yes, it took us a long time to learn to use our powers on them, to control them without killing them.* He laughed, a low grumble of a laugh that filled the chamber like the grumble the volcano often made when it irrupted. *But we have perfected it now, little Naga. We are ready. Get up. Don't make me drag you up, or it will hurt both of us.*

Shaking, the Naga drew himself up onto his hind legs. Waves of emotion from his dragon self ripped through him: lust for power to control, use, and feed on the humans. To rule the world and make every creature kneel at his feet. And the Naga's own emotions rolled back through his dragon self: betrayal, hate, anger, a gnawing desire for revenge. The humans abhorred him. His own family had tried to kill him, and would have succeeded if he hadn't been able to twist their minds at the last moment. He still might have died if his dragon self had not been so close by and heard his desperate mental call for help. How he hated his family. His steel claws clicked as he imagined tearing through the tender flesh of their human hides, devouring them body and bone. They would pay…he would make them pay for what they did to him.

*You cannot go to the humans like this*, his dragon self said. *You must clean up and change your clothes.*

His dragon self forced his Naga self over to the corner of the cavern where he nested. He had a pile of blankets where he slept, a pool of hot water to wash and drink, a wooden chest where he kept his human things, and a large oval mirror on a stand that his dragon self had stolen from a human ship long ago. The Naga did not like the mirror. He did not like to see how human he looked reflected in the smooth silver surface. But his dragon self forced him to go stand in front of the mirror. He tried to look away, but his dragon self took control of his movements and forced him to stare at himself and take in every detail: His clothes slicked with blood from his dinner feast. The steel claws strapped to his hands. His flaming blond hair, so dirty and matted it looked like the sooty magma cooling on his dragon self.

*You are human,* his dragon self said.

*No, we are dragon,* the Naga answered.

*I am dragon, you are human.* His dragon self shoved the Naga into a burning pool of old memories then clawed their minds apart.

The Naga fell to his knees, screaming, and pressed his hands to his head as the memories of his childhood seared him. He lived in a comfortable home with a family. Dressed like a human. Ate like a human. Spoke their language. Trained in his father's profession to work along-side him someday. He thought they loved him, cared for him; he was their own flesh and blood until...the dragon sickness had taken him. Their reaction had been swift and brutal. They tried to kill him, without even telling him why. No explanation, no warning, just betrayal and death.

The Naga sprang to his feet, growling. He flung open his chest and grabbed the sword that lay inside. The finest steel, perfectly balanced, and he'd trained long and hard to use it when he was young. He unsheathed it and turned to the mirror. Even after so many decades he still looked like a youth.

*But you are old enough now,* his dragon self growled into his mind. *See, you've even grown a beard finally.*

The Naga gagged. The image in the mirror looked so much like the memory of his father. Younger yes, but with the beard, which had only started to grow in the last half a decade, the man in the glass could very well be the same who had tried to murder him.

The Naga shouted and swung the sword at the mirror.

The sword cleaved through the wooden frame and shattered the glass. The impact of the strike felt good and solid through the hilt against the palms of his hands. The crash and tinkle of glass filled the Naga with joy. Destroy. Kill. Avenge. He was not human. He was rage.

*But you must pretend to be human for a while if you want your revenge*, his dragon self said.

*Yes, of course.* The Naga kicked the shards of glass out of his way. *Where is that silver wyrm?*

His dragon self roared and the silver serpent sulked into the room, carrying a bundle of human clothes. Her mind twisted in rebellion, but the Naga crushed those thoughts and sent a spike of pain into her mind as punishment.

The serpent whimpered and dropped the bundle at the Naga's feet.

*Go, get the boat ready*, his dragon self ordered the serpent. She scrambled away while the Naga unbuckled the claws from his hands. He rinsed them in the pool of water and then tossed them into the chest. "I suppose I can't take them with me," he muttered aloud. His voice sounded strange to him. He was no longer used to human speech.

*You must use the clothing Silverwave has brought for you*, his dragon self said.

Reluctantly the Naga peeled the bloody clothes from his body then eased himself into the warm water. It loosened his aching muscles but took a disturbingly long amount of time for him to wash the dirt and dried blood out of his hair, and even longer to comb out the tangles, but his dragon self made him do it. When he finished, he dried and put on the human clothes. Brown cotton trousers and white shirt. Brown bovinder leather boots. The Naga's mouth twisted in disgust. *There, do I look human enough for you?* he asked his dragon self.

*Say that out loud in human speech.*

"There, do I look like a human now?" the Naga yelled.

His dragon self licked his cruel teeth. *Human enough to eat.*

The Naga snorted and buckled on his sword.

*You will do everything just the way we planned*, his dragon self said.

"Yes, of course. We will meet again at Stonefountain as rulers of the world." The Naga left the chamber and followed a long tunnel down into a grotto where Silverwave waited beside a small wooden boat that his dragon self had stolen from the Maranies. He checked to make sure Silverwave had stocked it as ordered with enough food and water to see him across the ocean from the secluded Eastern Isle where he lived to the east coast of Maran.

*There is a hooded cloak there also*, Silverwave said, *to keep the sun from burning your face. You will need it. You've lived underground for too long. Your skin is not used to the sun, especially at the intensity as it glares off the water.*

The Naga stared at the serpent. His dragon self had not ordered her to get the cloak. She must be trying to rebel in some way. She often did. But he sensed only concern for his welfare. *What cause do you have to care if I burn in the sun?* he snapped at her.

Silverwave lowered her head and slipped into the water without answering.

*Fine, keep your secrets you little wyrm. You know I could tear them from your mind if I wished.* His dragon self would do it without hesitation, but that part of him had separated their minds for a time so he could think like a human. A necessary evil with where he was headed and what he intended to do. He was surprised that he had no desire to torment the silver serpent further. It wasn't worth the effort as long as she obeyed his commands. He climbed into the boat even though a nagging part of him screamed that she had done something nice for him, and no one did anything nice for him without hurting him for it in the end.

Silverwave slipped into a harness that connected her to the boat.

The Naga loosed the boat from shore, and Silverwave shot forward, dragging the boat from the grotto and out into the open ocean. Sunlight beat down on him. He grabbed the cloak and flung it over himself. The light cotton fabric smelled like the Varnan desert. He choked and battled to keep the memories of his childhood from overwhelming him again.

"What have you done?" he yelled at the serpent. "Are you trying to poison me?" He thrust the cloak aside and buried his face in his hands.

Silverwave made no reply. When he probed her mind again, he found only concern for his welfare. He would need the cloak. The sun would burn him.

*I'm used to burns*, he snapped at her, all too aware of the ugly scars that covered so much of his body. Not his face, thank the Fountain. His dragon self had never burned his hands or face. He needed them, after all, to execute the plan.

The ocean swells rocked the boat, making the Naga queasy, but the serpent pulled him on a straight course faster than any sail or oar could have. The island disappeared behind him, leaving only the undulating array of blues and greens of the water and the bright sun reflecting off it in his eyes. In less than an hour his tender skin felt like it was on fire. Reluctantly he pulled the cloak back over himself and shaded his face. When the memories threatened to overwhelm him, he locked them away behind shield after shield: stone walls and iron bars and mountains and oceans and rivers of lava. The only memory he kept free was that of his betrayal.

The thought of vengeance sustained him day and night all through his ocean crossing. After what seemed like an eternity on the water, the Maran coast finally came into sight.

"Where are we?" he asked the silver serpent as she pulled him ashore on an isolated spit of sand below a rocky cliff.

*Longshire, Eastland Province. Most of the land here has been cleared of trees for farming. I took the clothes you wear from a farm near here.*

"Any path up these cliffs?"

*Yes, that cleft there to the right. It's a bit steep at first, but then it becomes easy to traverse. Can I return to my home now? You have no further use for me.* Silverwave slipped out of the harness and inched toward the water that lapped against the sand in gentle waves.

"No. I still need you. Stay close to the Maran coast, and meet me at Wareham when I call."

Silverwave tried to rebel, but the Naga bent her will to his own before he let her slide back into the ocean. When she'd gone, he climbed the cleft up into the human lands. Farm fields spread out before him, dressed in green. He found a road and followed it toward a small town. But he did not go into town. He hid behind a stone fence and watched the wooden houses with their stone chimneys that smoked and filled the air with smells he hadn't experienced in a long time. Hot bread baking, and pies, and stew. He'd forgotten that humans cooked their food, that there even was food beyond raw meat. His stomach grumbled. He hissed in annoyance and ignored it, watching instead to see the people who lived in these human habitations. They came and went: men, women, children. But he saw none that would be right for his needs.

Stomach complaining, he abandoned the town and trudged out toward the scattered farm houses.

It took him two days to find the person he needed. A young farmer, twenty-one years old, with blond hair close to the shade of the Naga's, and about his same height. Their faces were not the same, or course, but close enough.

He set upon the farmer when he was alone in the fields. The farmer's mind was easy to trap and control. The Naga pressed his hand against the farmer's forehead and consumed all his knowledge: every memory, every experience, every emotion, and every personality trait. The man's name was Edward of Longshire, a noble name for a mewling farmer. The Naga finished him with his sword and buried his bones in the newly turned soil so no one would find the body. Then the Naga donned the farmer's cap and returned to the farm house to deal with the farmer's family.

When he flung open the door, the farmer's wife, Cynthia, froze with a bowl of cake batter in her hands. The spoon she'd been stirring with slipped through her fingers.

"Who are you?" she asked. "Why are you wearing Edward's cap?"

The Naga spread his hands. "Cynthia, my love, I am Edward." He slid into her mind, careful not to crush it— he'd practiced long to be able to do this right—and twisted her memories just enough that every thought she'd ever had of Edward matched his new face. In her mind, he was

Edward, the boy she'd grown up hating, the young man she'd fallen in love with, and the husband she'd devoted her life to.

"You're home early," she said, returning to her cake making.

"Yes, my love." Edward always called her that, though it made the Naga nearly gag. He would never let himself love anyone. "I've decided I no longer want to be a farmer. There is an election coming up soon, and I plan on running for the Maran Senate. Don't you think I would make a good senator?"

"But Edward."

"I will be a senator, and you will be happy for me," Edward, the Naga, said. Cynthia's mind was powerless to resist his direct command.

"Yes of course, Edward. We should talk to my father about this, and yours."

"I quite intend to. Let's invite the whole family over for dinner to make the announcement."

Within a few days, the whole family accepted the Naga as Edward and agreed to help him get elected to the senate. Within a week, the entire town did as well. Two months later, with the unanimous backing of all of Longshire, Edward became a Maran senator.

# Chapter One

**Kanvar paced in front** of the arched window at the edge of his and Dharanidhar's chamber in the golden palace. Dhar slept curled up on the rock floor. He'd slept a lot since they'd straggled back from Darvat. Parmver insisted he needed time to rest and heal before rejoining the blue dragon pride. Kanvar knew that was true. There were so many young blues anxious to challenge him for right to lead, and Dhar was old. How many more fights to the death could he and Kanvar survive?

Kanvar gritted his teeth and ran his hand over his blue dragonscale armor. With the helm and gauntlets, it would protect him from dragon fire, unless it hit him full in the face. He and Dhar had learned from their first fight that Kanvar was their most vulnerable point. Of course, Grandfather Raza had needed to help Kanvar make the gauntlet for his deformed left hand. Kanvar clenched his thumb and two fingers into a tiny fist. At least he'd fashioned the boot for his twisted left foot himself. He was ready to fight any blue dragon that challenged Dharanidhar.

Dhar let out a sleepy snort and filled the chamber with a rumbling snore. Kanvar sighed, wishing Dhar would wake up and fly him somewhere, anywhere.

At least Frost was safe. The females of the pride had taken her under their wings and pampered her like the delicate creature she was. Denali missed her, but Amar would not allow any of the gold dragons to fly him up there. Until Dhar recovered fully, Denali and Kanvar were both stuck in the palace. At least Denali liked the palace. Kanvar could not say the same for himself.

He stared through the window down to the jungle. The day was clear of clouds, so the dense green canopy was visible far below. So far he could barely hear the screech of the black monkeys and cries of the scaly macaws. Kanvar returned to limping back and forth in front of the window. He had to get out of this place before he went crazy.

In the back of his mind he was aware of the other Nagas and dragons at the palace, busy with their writings and studies. Kanvar balled his good hand into a fist and growled under his breath. That's all these gold dragons seemed to want to do—write, study, read, compose music and poetry, paint and sculpt. Could life possibly get more boring?

Bensharie, the Great Gold Dragon King's youngest son, sensed Kanvar's awareness sweep over him and looked up from the poem he'd been composing. He fluttered his golden wings. *What's wrong, My Prince?*

*Nothing, Bensharie, go back to your insipid poetry.* If Kanvar had not bonded with Dharanidhar, Bensharie would have taken the bond, even if it meant becoming crippled along with Kanvar. Kanvar appreciated that. Of all the gold dragons, Kanvar liked Bensharie the best, but the two of them were very different from each other.

Bensharie set down his quill pen and flapped away from the table where he'd been working.

Kanvar closed his mind off from the dragon and went to his corner of the chamber. It was richly decorated with a gold and red rug, depicting Stonefountain at the height of its glory. Kanvar went to a chest at the foot of his bed, and ran his fingers over the carvings in the ancient wood. The scene depicted there told a different story than the rug: dragons chained as slaves and humans living in deplorable poverty. Akshara, the Great Blue Liberator, had carved this chest and others like it that Dharanidhar and Kanvar had inherited after Akshara died.

Stonefountain, Kanvar had stopped there briefly on his way to Darvat. The scream of the shattered fountain still haunted his memory. That, and the knowledge that the fountain could be healed. But at what cost? Returning all the missing singing stones to the fountain may set the suffering spirits to rest, but then there would be nothing to keep the Nagas from controlling and enslaving people.

Kanvar stared back and forth between the rug and the chest. What if the fountain could be healed? What if the bright civilization of Stonefountain could be rebuilt with all the knowledge and wonders it once had? What if the old wrongs could be righted? If there was only some way that the Nagas could be trusted to live safely with other humans and dragons. But Kanvar couldn't see how without the balance the singing stones created by their existence.

He opened the chest and pulled out the crossbow his grandfather Raza had made for him. It was lighter and sturdier than the one Kanvar had purchased at the Maran colony. A hand crank on the side made it easier for Kanvar to cock and load. He'd practiced with it enough he could arm the weapon between one breath and the next. Rajahansa, the Great Gold Dragon King, had scolded him twice already for setting up a target to practice with inside the palace. Like it was really hurting anything? The palace was so big it shouldn't matter to anyone if Kanvar shot his crossbow in his own chamber.

Kanvar settled for polishing the wooden stalk.

The flap of wings sounded outside the window.

Kanvar looked up and saw a blur of sunlight.

*May I come in?* Bensharie asked.

*I suppose.* Kanvar watched Bensharie become visible as he glided into the shadow of the chamber. Bensharie landed with a small click of his claws against the rock and looked nervously over at the sleeping blue dragon, fearing he might have wakened him.

"If only," Kanvar muttered. He'd like nothing more than for Dharanidhar to wake, stretch, and insist it was time to be gone from the palace.

Bensharie skirted Dharanidhar and came over to where Kanvar sat with his crossbow. *Good morning, Highness,* he said with a bow.

"Morning, Bensharie." Kanvar rubbed the polishing cloth along the blue dragon carved into the stalk of the crossbow.

*My father thinks Devaj might return today.* Bensharie folded his wings and lay down so his face was level with Kanvar's.

"That would be nice."

Devaj had been sent as an emissary from the palace to Karishi. Kanvar had wanted to go, but his father insisted he should stay with his dragon, besides he'd traveled enough already, going to Darvat with Raahi. Not that his father should have any say where Kanvar went.

*Well, he is the king,* Bensharie said.

Kanvar grimaced. "Your king maybe. I never swore fealty to him. Dharanidhar and I are free to come and go as we choose."

*It seems Dharanidhar is choosing to stay. Can you blame him? He is old, blind, and injured? He's succeeded in driving the Maranies from Kundiland like he vowed he would after they killed his mate. He's earned a restful and quiet life. If he stays here, he need not fight with the young blue dragons, or hunt for food, or fly off into the middle of a hurricane.*

"How dare you?" Kanvar rose to his feet with a white-knuckle grip on his crossbow. Good thing it wasn't loaded or he might consider shooting Bensharie in the foot.

Bensharie cocked his head to the side and narrowed his eyes at Kanvar. *It's the truth. You shouldn't take it personally.*

Kanvar glanced over at his sleeping friend. "Dhar flew willingly into the hurricane because we needed to save Raahi's people from slavery. He would die in the defense of freedom. Any blue dragon would."

*Not any blue dragon. None of the other Great Blue dragons did, in fact. You and Dhar flew off alone without the rest of the pride. If he had invited them to join him in his quest to the other side of the world, would they have come? I think not. Dharanidhar is the only Great dragon hero of our time. I have written several poems and two songs about him.* Bensharie ruffled his wings and bowed to the sleeping blue dragon, then once more to Kanvar. *So, you see, I mean no offense to you or him, Kanvar, when I point out the fact that he is old and hurt and has earned a quiet retirement here at the palace.*

Kanvar fingered his crossbow. "I'm too young to retire. I can't just sit around the palace and do nothing."

*You could try writing poetry or take up painting. You should spend more time with Parmver. He has a lot that he can teach you. Of the three fundamentals—communicating, manipulating, and summoning— what have you learned so far?*

"Nothing interesting," Kanvar snapped. "He refuses to teach me anything fun. Not even easy manipulation like levitating or shaping gold. I asked him to teach me summoning. He refused. Said I was too young and need to focus solely on communicating. I might hurt myself if I try anything more." Anger welled up in Kanvar. He'd argued with Parmver about it several times, but Parmver was adamant, Kanvar had to learn to control his mind before learning anything else. "Besides, I am a dragon hunter, not a stodgy old man whose mind is filled with tonics and tinctures. I have got to get out of this prison."

Bensharie spread his wings and stepped back away from Kanvar. *This palace is not a prison.*

"It is to me."

*I could fly you down to the jungle village.*

"Raahi's not there anymore."

*But there are other humans you could spend time with. You could go hunting, I suppose, though why you would want to kill a living creature I can't imagine.*

Kanvar took a deep breath. "You're trying to be friendly, aren't you? And I'm being ornery as usual. Forgive me, I guess I'm not as nice as Devaj or my father."

Bensharie snorted. *Few beings are. Shall I take you to the village?*

A weight lifted from Kanvar's chest. "I'd like that a lot." He smiled and grabbed his crossbow bolts and other hunting gear.

Though Bensharie was far smaller than Dharanidhar, Kanvar fit comfortably with his body settled between the dragon's wings, and his legs hanging on either side of Bensharie's neck. The gold dragon's plates formed a natural seat there, and when Bensharie lifted his head to take off, a plate on his neck fit down snugly overtop Kanvar's lap, holding him in place so he couldn't fall in flight. It was almost as if the Great Gold dragons had been created for flight with the Nagas. The flight was smooth and beautiful, and Kanvar pondered for a moment as the wind brushed his cheeks what his life might have been like if he had bonded with Bensharie. If he hadn't needed to save Devaj from the Great Blue dragons, if they could have known for sure Bensharie wouldn't be crippled by the bond, if they'd grown up together in the palace.

Useless thoughts. Kanvar's life had been a brutal struggle to survive, and Bensharie had no part of that.

Bensharie glided down to land on the rock shelf in the cliff above the jungle village. He lowered his head, releasing the plate that held Kanvar in place. Kanvar slid off and rubbed Bensharie's shoulder. "Thank you, Bensharie. Come back for me when Devaj returns, all right?"

*Certainly, My Prince.* Bensharie took flight, vanishing as a ripple in the golden sunlight. Kanvar started down the narrow steps to the village. Step, limp, step, limp. It took him far longer than any other person, but he was glad to be moving, doing, going anywhere however difficult, rather than sitting in his father's gilded prison.

Tana met him on the platform at the bottom of the stairs. Her black hair hung loose around the pearly gray skin of her face. Her eyes twinkled with joy at seeing him. She wore her usual shirt and trousers of mottled green that her people used to blend into the jungle, but even that could not hide the subtle curves of her feminine body. Kanvar flushed as she wrapped him in a welcoming hug.

"Kanvar, I'm glad you came." Tana took his hand and steadied him across the wide branch that formed a pathway over to the next platform. She continued talking as they went. "You've been gone so long, and I've been worried about you and Raahi. How did your trip to Darvat go? Did you find Raahi's family and save them? How long are you going to stay? A while, I hope, this time. There's something I've been wanting to talk to you about, only I don't know how to say it, and I'm kind of scared so maybe perhaps you could listen and not laugh at me."

He sensed a swirl of worries in her mind but kept his shields up. Whatever she wanted to talk about, he'd let her say it aloud.

They reached the round hut that was Tana's own. Kanvar let her lead him inside and they both settled onto a mat on the floor. She took up a bowl of nuts that waited there and began shelling them. Kanvar watched her work for a moment without saying anything.

"I miss Raahi," Tana said into the silence. "Is he all right?"

"He's fine." Kanvar fumbled with where to put his hand. He wished he could hold Tana's with it, but hers were busy with the nuts.

"He's fine? That's all you're going to tell me? You fly off to the other side of the world, and the best you can say is he's fine?" Tana crushed one of the nuts so hard the shell shattered and flew across the hut in a dozen pieces.

Kanvar laughed. "I'm sorry, Tana. It's a long, crazy story."

"Then tell it."

Tana finished shelling all the nuts before Kanvar reached the end of his story with Raahi's triumphant parade around Huayna.

"You see, Tana, he's fine. A hero in fact. But he had to stay there with his family, didn't he?" Kanvar rubbed his sweaty hand on his leg, which made no difference since his gauntlet trapped the sweat against his skin. "But I miss him too. I guess I'll have to go hunting by myself now."

"I could come with you."

"You're a girl."

"Girls can hunt. No one says they can't. I bet some of the best dragon hunters who ever lived were women."

Kanvar grinned. "You're probably right. But do you want to, really. I mean, you won't get in trouble for it will you?"

Tana stood and tipped the broken shells out the back window so they tumbled toward the jungle floor below. "I'm old enough I can do as I like. Besides, no one will stop me from spending time with the Naga prince now will they?"

"Great." Kanvar pulled himself to his feet. His mind spun, trying to think of the best hunt he could take Tana on. Something close to the village in case Devaj did come back today. He headed outside and over to the lift that would let them down to the jungle floor.

Tana stayed behind in the hut for a moment then came out carrying a long jungle knife. The villagers used the sharp blades for chopping through vines and under-brush when they traveled along the jungle floor. Kanvar supposed it would work just as well on a serpent or dragon, but he suddenly didn't feel like killing anything. Perhaps Bensharie's feelings had rubbed off on him as he flew, or more likely, he didn't want to do anything unsavory in Tana's presence.

She joined him on the lift and untied the rope with the counterweight that allowed them to descend smoothly to the base of the trees.

"So, what are we after," Tana said as they strolled along a trail through the underbrush.

Kanvar drew his crossbow from his back, cocked it, and loaded a bolt into the slot just in case they ran into trouble. "Jewel dragonflies,"

"What? You can't call those dragons."

"They are dragons, and valuable ones at that. Near im-possible to catch too, unless you know what you're doing."

"Or you have a net."

"We don't have a net."

"I can go back and get one. Come on, children catch jewel dragonflies for fun. We could hunt a lesser green serpent. There are plenty of them around here."

"Go ahead. There's one there, on that tree, see it?" He pointed to a six foot wingless green serpent that had curled itself around a low branch just off the trail.

"That kind's not even poisonous," Tana said.

"A dragon does not have to be poisonous or ferocious to be worth something."

"You're just saying that because I'm a girl."

"No, I'm not. It's the first and most important thing my father ever taught me. The most accomplished dragon hunting isn't glamorous or dangerous. You make more money and live to spend it if you hunt smart. That green serpent there is big enough for two sets of fashionable shoes that the Maranies will snap up like sweet nectar. But those serpents are fast, you'll have a time of it trying to take it with the jungle knife. I'd even have a hard time hitting it with my crossbow."

"Its eyes are closed. It's sleeping."

"No. It's listening to us. It knows exactly where we are and what we're doing. If I take a step off this path, it will be gone like that." Kanvar snapped his fingers.

"You think I can't hunt. I'll have you know, I've spent more time in this jungle then you ever will. I live here. You're just a visitor."

Kanvar's gut twisted. He had not meant to make Tana mad at him, he'd just been telling her what he'd learned from his father and grandfather. "Tana, I'm—"

"Shut up." She spun the jungle knife in her hand then threw it. It flashed through the air and sliced through the serpent's neck as it buried itself in the woody branch. "Shoes. People make shoes out of this lousy critter."

She strode over to the tree, jerked her knife from the branch, and pulled the serpent's body loose, draping it over her shoulders.

"You can eat the meat too. It tastes pretty good," Kanvar said, trying to sound smart, but the look Tana gave him let him know that the youngest toddler in the village could have said as much.

"You're a dragon hunter. I thought that meant you hunted dragons, big ones, dangerous ones, like that Great Green that tried to eat me, or the Great Blue dragon you killed to free your brother."

"Great dragons are people. Killing them is murder, unless you're fighting to defend yourself from them." Kanvar shuddered, remembering the feeling of emptiness and loss he'd experienced when the Great dragons he'd killed had died.

"I've got an idea," Tana said. "I've seen tracks of some large dragon down the river out close by the Maran colony. Claw marks a good three feet across. Let's go see if we can find out what kind of dragon it is. If it's not a Great dragon, I say we take it." Tana strode off down the path along the river.

Kanvar followed, though he had no chance of keeping up with her at that speed.

She stopped and waited for him every once in a while. Then set off again as soon as he caught up with her. The river gurgled along beside him, the inky water making its way sluggishly out to the ocean. He hoped it wasn't Indumauli's tracks Tana had encountered. He reached out with his mind in search of Indumauli.

*Kanvar, what brings you to the river?* Indumauli's cool thoughts trickled into Kanvar's mind.

*Hunting with Tana. Is there a big dragon down this way?*

A sharp hiss from Indumauli knifed through his mind. Kanvar winced. *What? What is it?* he asked.

*A lesser volcanic red dragon. It landed by the river a week ago. Haven't seen one around here for a long time. One of the volcanoes must be stirring. You should not hunt such a creature. Your crossbow bolts will not penetrate its magma-encrusted scales.*

"By the fountain," Kanvar swore and broke into a limping run. Tana was ahead of him somewhere out of sight. "Tana!" he yelled. "Tana, come back!"

A troop of black monkeys screamed at him in response. But Tana did not answer. She'd gone too far ahead.

*Tana*, he called with his mind, searching for her consciousness amidst all the dizzying animals in the jungle around him. *Tana, can you hear me? Stay away from the dragon. We can't take this one.*

Tana's piercing scream rose above the other jungle sounds. The black monkeys fell silent. A flock of birds took to the sky. Even the hum of the insects stilled. Kanvar's mind snapped toward the sound and made con-tact with Tana's.

# Dragonbound IV

The volcanic dragon had trapped her beneath its massive claw. She hacked at it, but the jungle knife chipped and broke against the black stone that encased its cooled body. It roared, and heat rippled from the burning red fire at the back of its throat. Lava trickled like saliva from its mouth, the drops just missing Tana's face as it bent toward her.

# Chapter Two

*Dharanidhar,* **Kanvar screamed** into his friend's mind, dragging him awake from a sound sleep. *Dhar, I need your help right now.* Dhar was big enough he might be able to tear the lesser volcanic dragon into rocky bits.

Dhar rose and spread his wings, but hesitated. *You are my eyes, Kanvar. I can't see to fly to you. There are mountains between us.*

*There's a dragon. It has Tana. A red volcanic dragon. I can't fight it alone.* Kanvar continued his limping run at top speed toward Tana and the dragon.

*Then stay away from it.*

*It will kill her.*

*Better her than us.*

*You don't mean that.*

Dhar growled in frustration. He wished with all his heart he could come to Kanvar's aid.

Water splashed in the river beside Kanvar. *I'm with you,* Indumauli said. *Though I don't know how much use I'll be. My fangs won't penetrate that creature's armor.*

Kanvar pushed through the underbrush, raced around a tree trunk, and came face to face with the volcanic dragon. On four legs its shoulder stood eight feet high. Its red scales were covered with black volcanic rock and could only be seen through a network of cracks across its body. Its eyes glowed red as it tore the dead green serpent from Tana's shoulders and devoured it.

"Hey!" Kanvar yelled, lifting his crossbow. "Get away from my girl."

The dragon raised its head to stare at Kanvar with burning eyes. It roared and spat a ball of red fire at him.

Kanvar turned so the fire flashed against the back of his blue dragonscale armor. Red dragon fire, not as hot as blue dragon fire, but still hot enough to singe the stray hairs sticking out from his helm. And his hair had just barely grown back after his encounter with the volcano in the Great North. After the blast, Kanvar twisted back around, took aim, and sent a crossbow bolt into the dragon's maw. His aim was true, but the bolt melted in the furnace at the back of the dragon's throat.

The dragon belched and growled.

The earth gave way beneath the dragon's claw that held Tana pinned against the ground. While Kanvar had kept the dragon's attention, Indumauli had dug through the riverbank to get to Tana. The ground collapsed beneath her as Indumauli got his coils around her and dragged her into the water and away from Kanvar and the dragon.

Kanvar took a step back, but the dragon leaped into the air above him and spat another ball of fire toward his face.

He twisted away and limped toward the water, but the dragon dropped to the ground between him and the river, blocking his escape.

Kanvar grabbed another crossbow bolt and got it into place. He aimed and fired just as the dragon blew another ball of fire at him. The bolt passed through the fire and hit the dragon in the eye. Kanvar turned his face away from the blast and loaded his crossbow once more. When he turned back to shoot the dragon in the other eye, he found Bensharie hovering beside a surprisingly happy volcanic dragon. It sagged to the ground and started humming to itself. Bensharie hit it once more with his sparkling joy breath, then tore the crossbow bolt from its eye. The volcanic red dragon burbled and wandered off into the jungle.

*By the fountain, what are you thinking?* Bensharie said to Kanvar. *You're a Naga. Why didn't you just make him walk away? You didn't have to hurt him.*

Kanvar lowered his crossbow and wiped the sweat out of his eyes with is stumpy left hand. The smell of his singed hair made him gag. "I don't use my powers to control people's minds," he snapped.

*Oh, so blinding a creature or killing it is better than sending it happily on its way?*

Kanvar growled under his breath and limped off in search of Indumauli and Tana.

*Kanvar,* Bensharie said.

"Leave me alone."

*Devaj has returned.*

"Great. If *he* wants to talk to me, I'll be at the village."

*He brought Karishi with him.*

"I don't care." Kanvar blocked Bensharie's thoughts from his mind. Shame filled him as Bensharie flew away. Bensharie was right, even though Kanvar didn't want to admit it. He should have just used his powers to make the volcanic dragon want to leave Tana alone. But he hadn't thought of that. It was a stupid, stupid mistake, and Tana could have died because of it.

"Kanvar." A very wet Tana enveloped him in a soggy hug. "Was that fun or what? I want to hunt dragons with you every day."

Kanvar tried to protest, but Tana took his hand. Maybe it was worth facing a lesser volcanic dragon if he got to spend time with her. "All right. But I think we should go back to the village now. I've had as much excitement as I can take for one day."

Tana laughed. "One lesser volcanic dragon and you're spent? I might think you were a helpless little crippled boy if I didn't know better."

Kanvar flushed, pulled his hand away from her, and limped back toward the village. Perhaps he should have gone with Bensharie.

Tana caught up with him, grabbed his hand once more, and dragged him to a stop. River water dripped down her cheeks, and her lips quivered. "I was joking, Kanvar. That dragon scared the breath out of me, but I'm trying to be brave because I know you are. You didn't even flinch when it blew those fire balls at you."

"Oh, believe me, I flinched." Kanvar's throat was raw from the heat of the fire.

Tana reached out and rubbed her fingers along the melted hair that stuck out from his dragonscale helmet. "Good thing you have armor." She pressed her shivering wet body against his chest. "And it's still warm."

Kanvar eased his crossbow into its harness on his back and put his good arm around her. His heart beat faster than it had a few moments before when he'd fought the dragon. "Tana I—"

She pressed a finger against his lips to silence him. "I need to tell you something, Kanvar. Only, I don't know how to say it. I'm frightened."

"The dragon's gone. It can't hurt you now. Even if it came back, I wouldn't let it." He stroked her hair and let a little bit of reassurance from his own mind seep into hers. Parmver *had* been teaching him how to use his communicating powers safely without forcing his will on other people. She could accept his reassurance or not.

"It's not just about that dragon, at least not completely." She shuddered in his arm. "Yes, that dragon. I knew how to find it, felt where it was, but there…there are other dragons too. I can feel them in my mind. I don't know how to explain it. Sometimes I dream that I'm a dragon. My thoughts are starting to get mixed up all the time." She rubbed her forehead and let her dark imploring eyes meet his.

Kanvar's chest tightened and his throat constricted so he could hardly speak. "Tana—"

"Please, Kanvar. You can't tell anyone. I don't want them to think I'm crazy. If you could just help me straighten my mind out. You're a Naga, you can do that, right?"

"Of course I can." He kissed her forehead, drew her gently against his chest, and put up a shield around her mind, blocking out the thoughts of all the other creatures in the jungle, everything but his own reassuring presence. "Better?"

Tana gasped and tensed, then slowly relaxed. "Yes, better. But now I feel empty. What did you do?"

Kanvar swallowed. "I shielded your mind. How old are you, Tana?"

"Almost seventeen."

"How long have you been feeling the dragons so intensely?"

She shivered and ran her fingers down his scaly armor. "A few months, well…I've always felt them a little, in a hazy sort of way, but now they're all tangled up in my mind."

He leaned down and pressed his cheek against her forehead. Her skin felt cool against his own. "You don't have a fever yet."

She flinched away, pulling out of his arm. "What do you mean? What are you saying?"

"You're not crazy, Tana. You're a Naga. I felt the same way before I met Dhar and came down with the dragon sickness."

"No. I can't be. Parmver came to the village. He tested all of us children and chose Aadi to be the Naga. Not me." Tana crossed her arms over her chest and stumbled along the trail beside the river.

"Parmver doesn't choose who gets to be a Naga. He just looks for those he thinks might be. He can't really tell for sure until someone comes down with the fever." Kanvar pushed himself to catch up with her and get his arm around her, pulling her close to him once more. "Don't be frightened, Tana. Everything is going to be all right."

The heavy flap of dragon wings drowned out her reply, and Elkatran, Devaj's Great Gold dragon settled into the shade of the trees, his wings barely fitting in the opening of the canopy along the river. He landed on the riverbank close to Kanvar and Tana, and Devaj slid down from his neck.

"Hey, little brother. Bensharie sends his apology for interrupting your hunt. He says he recons you were just trying to show off for the human girl." Devaj lifted his eyebrows and grinned. "Looks like you succeeded."

Fear raced through Tana. Fear and respect for the older of the two princes. She tried to pull away from Kanvar, but he held her gently in place. "It's all right, Tana.

I have an idea, how would you like to come with me to visit the golden palace? It's amazing."

"I-I can't. Only Nagas are allowed there."

"Oh, I think I could bring a friend home if I want. Father's not going to stop me, is he, Devaj?" Kanvar speared Devaj with a look that warned he better go along with Kanvar or he'd regret it. Kanvar wanted to shout the good news to his brother that Tana was a Naga, but she'd begged him not to tell anyone before confiding in him. He wouldn't need to say anything though. They'd all know it as soon as she came down with the fever, especially if she was already at the palace.

Devaj shifted uncomfortably. "I don't know, Kanvar. Karishi is here, and His Majesty has called a solemn meeting of the Naga council. I've been sent to fetch you. Now's not really a good time for...courting."

"Courting?" Tana pulled away from Kanvar and look-ed wide-eyed from one brother to the other. "We're not. It's not like that." She pushed past Kanvar and sprinted up the trail toward the village.

Kanvar glared at his brother. "You are so going to regret that, Devaj." Kanvar turned his back and limped off after Tana.

It only took Devaj two steps to catch up with him, grab his shoulders, and spin him around. "You have been summoned to a meeting. We have to go now."

Kanvar punched Devaj in the stomach and twisted out of his grasp. "Leave me alone, Devaj. I can't leave her. Not now. Not when she's so close to…so vulnerable." Kanvar continued up the path.

"What are you talking about? She's headed to the village. She's safe enough."

"No she's not. She's…she won't stay there. She's looking for dragons. By the fountain, she almost got eaten by a volcanic dragon just now because she went looking for it. She felt it, Devaj. She felt the dragon and went looking, and I'm trying to shield her mind, but I can't do it if she gets too far away." Kanvar tried to limp faster but Devaj matched his stride.

"What are you saying, Kanvar?"

"What I'm *not* saying is what she asked me not to tell anyone. But, Devaj, she needs to come to the palace. A stupid meeting can't get in the way of this. Believe me." Tana's mind slipped out of his grasp, and his shields around her dissipated. Kanvar paused, gasping for breath. She'd gotten too far ahead of him, and he could never move fast enough to catch her.

Devaj glanced up the path in the direction Tana had gone then back to Kanvar. "She's a Naga?"

"You go get her," Kanvar said. "You're faster than I am, but she's afraid of you, so be careful, be nice. Somehow you have to get her to trust you."

Devaj bolted down the path. *Don't worry. Nice is my specialty. Go back to Elkatran and meet me at the cliff.*

Kanvar took a deep breath and then limped back to the river and the Great Gold dragon.

*Your face is red*, Elkatran said, bending down so Kanvar could climb onto his neck. *Is it because you are breathing hard or because your face is burned?*

"No idea."

Elkatran's tongue snaked out and slathered saliva across Kanvar's face.

"Ugh. Gross," Kanvar said, but he didn't wipe the healing fluid off until his face stopped burning.

Elkatran lifted from the ground and twisted so he could get back into the sky between the trees.

It only took a couple of minutes for Elkatran to fly to the shelf in the cliff. Kanvar laughed at his memory of the first time he'd come to the cliff, bound and struggling, terrified that the villagers meant to cast him down to his death because he was a Naga.

Sunlight glimmered off the gong that still hung from the rock, waiting for the villagers to strike it and signal to the Naga King that a new Naga had come down with the dragon sickness. That gong had waited silent for hundreds of years, but it had rung for Kanvar. He considered jumping from Elkatran's neck and ringing it again now for Tana, but doubted she'd appreciate the gesture.

An hour passed before Devaj appeared at the top of the stairs followed by Tana and her father, the village chief.

Kanvar slipped down from Elkatran's neck and went over to Tana. "Are you all right? I..." He looked over at Devaj. "I didn't tell him anything. He just..."

Goose bumps prickled Tana's arms, and her face looked sickly. She shook her head and backed away from Kanvar.

"Tana, believe me, this is a great honor," her father said. Kanvar noted he not only wore his feathered crown but also had on a cloak of dazzling scaly macaw feathers as if this were some ceremonial occasion.

"I like it here." Tana spoke barely loud enough for any of them to hear her.

"Of course you do," Devaj said in a silky voice. "And you can come back here any time you want, to visit or to stay. Coming with us to the palace doesn't mean you're leaving anything behind. Do you worry the village will disappear when you go out to pick mushrooms? No, of course not, because you know it will be there when you come back just like it always has been."

"No one has *ever* come back from the palace," Tana said, this time her voice louder and more defiant.

"Nonsense. Kanvar comes back and forth all the time," Devaj said.

"He's different. He's not from the village."

Kanvar could tell that her argument was born of fear, not logic.

Her father took her arm and drew her over to Kanvar and Devaj. "No one has gone to the palace in generations, besides Aadi, so coming back or not isn't the issue. Tana, be reasonable. Go with the Nagas. They won't harm you."

"I-I don't think all three of us are going to fit on that gold dragon," Tana said. "No offense, but it's rather small isn't it?"

"Elkatran and I are still very young," Devaj said. "But don't worry. Their Majesties are on their way here and should arrive any moment."

Kanvar spread his mind out and realized that his father and Rajahansa were in fact just coming down to land. He could see the ripple of gold in the sunlight. Then a Great Gold dragon that dwarfed Elkatran appeared in the shadow of the cliffs and landed beside them. Kanvar backed away as his father dismounted and strode over to Tana and the village chieftain.

"Greetings, Jabari. Are you and yours well?"

Tana's father bowed. "All is well with us, Mighty One. Though my daughter, it seems, may need to join you. She is...unhappy about the prospect."

Kanvar's father was dressed in shimmering gold robes as usual and wore a gold crown across his brow. His sun-bronzed skin glimmered even in the shade of the cliffs. He gave Tana a gentle smile and took her hand. "I'm so pleased to meet you, Tana. Kanvar speaks so highly of you that I'm sure you will feel at home with us in no time at all."

Kanvar pressed his lips together and kept his mouth shut. In truth, he hadn't said anything to his father about Tana, but his father had often seen her in Kanvar's thoughts.

"Th-thank you, Majesty," Tana stuttered, overawed by his presence.

"Come, my dear. I will return you to your home and family as soon as possible."

Rajahansa reached out and took both of them in his hand, lifting them carefully up to his neck where Amar got her seated and secured. Then Rajahansa took to the air and swept away.

Kanvar let out a deep breath and rubbed his sweaty hand on his leg, which still did no good. The gauntlets might protect him from fire, but they could sure be a nuisance. "I don't think she's happy with me."

Devaj laughed. "She'll get over it. Come on, little brother. We need to get back too. There are important things to discuss, and I have a letter for you from General Chandran. Raahi said the general seemed quite agitated when he gave it to him to give to Karishi to hand off to you. Too bad we don't have a more direct way to communicate with him."

Kanvar's heart leaped and he wondered what had moved Chandran enough he was willing to try to contact the Nagas. He joined Devaj on Elkatran and headed back to the palace.

# Chapter Three

**Kanvar did not see** Tana when he landed at the palace with Devaj and Elkatran. His father had whisked her off into some chamber somewhere, and Devaj insisted Kanvar accompany him to the meeting hall.

They stepped into an oval chamber. At the center sat a table made from a silky black wood. A lace table cloth covered it, illuminated by a crystal chandelier that hung from the ceiling above. The table was set with sparkling white china that had a leafy gold pattern around the rim. Crystal goblets stood beside each of the eight place settings.

Kanvar limped over to the table and picked up one of the forks. It glimmered gold in his hand. "Isn't this just a bit excessive?" In all his time at the palace, he'd never bothered to attend one of the formal dinners, preferring to eat in his own chambers with Dharanidhar. "Do you know how much even one of these forks would be worth to most of the families in Daro?"

Devaj speared him with a stern look. "Actually, I do. I did grow up there the same as you. But do you realize what would happen to Daro's economy if we flooded it with gold? No, you don't, because you haven't studied economics, only dragon hunting."

Kanvar dropped the fork. "You're just angry because I slugged you in the gut."

Devaj laughed. He never had been able to stay stern or angry for long. "Little brother, someday you're going to learn that violence isn't the best answer for everything."

"It's worked all right so far. Besides, I'm bound to a Great Blue dragon. Violence is a way of life for them." Kanvar glanced around the empty chamber. "Where is everyone?"

"Well, Bellori is scrambling to reheat the food. Father is getting Tana settled in. Parmver is on his way. And Grandfather Raza—"

"Is right here." Kumar Raza strode into the room, dressed in casual cotton clothes rather than his red dragonscale armor.

"I thought you'd gone to the Varnan Colony to trade those dragon pelts you had," Kanvar said. He was pleased to see his grandfather. It would have been nice to have him there for the fight against the volcanic dragon.

"I've returned." Kumar strode over to Kanvar and pulled Kanvar's crossbow out of its harness. He ran his hand down the stalk, and his palm came away covered with black. "You scorched my crossbow? You do realize how hard I worked to make it."

Kanvar peeled his helmet off and dropped it on the table next to one of the plates. "I ran into a lesser volcanic dragon. Would have just avoided it, but it got hold of one of the village girls. Things got a little bit hot, but...everything turned out all right." He didn't want to admit to his grandfather that Bensharie had saved him. But then again, if Bensharie had not intervened Kanvar might have escaped from the volcanic dragon on his own.

"You escaped alive, you mean?" Kumar Raza said.

Kanvar nodded and accepted his crossbow as Raza handed it back to him. "Grandfather, how do you kill a volcanic red dragon? I can't figure out how I might have done it, even if I had a sword or a spear. Even if you could get past the magma and the scales, the inside is so hot it would melt the weapon before it could do any damage. You should have seen how fast it consumed my crossbow bolt. Hitting it in the eyes seemed the only option."

Kumar Raza shook his head. "You don't kill it, Kanvar. You stay away from it, and if that fails you trick it, or trap it, or distract it while you make your escape."

"But you killed at least two Great Red dragons, didn't you? You brought home one of the stones, and the red dragonscales for your armor. I remember that from when I was little. How did you do it?"

Kumar's brow furrowed and his eyes darkened. He turned away from Kanvar without answering and took a seat on the far side of the table. Before Kanvar could press him further, Parmver hobbled into the room, using his cane to help him walk as usual. His eyes widened as he took in Kanvar's fire-blackened armor. "Kanvar, lad," he said. "You're filthy, and your helmet is smudging the table cloth. Might I suggest you go clean up quickly before Rajahansa gets here? He won't be amused by your appearance."

"Rajahansa is never pleased by my appearance. I'm sure he'd be happier if I didn't exist at all." Kanvar scooped up his helmet and limped toward the arch that would lead back to his own chambers.

"Not true," Devaj called after him.

Parmver cleared his throat and called out to Kanvar as well. "Wake Dharanidhar and tell him he is invited also. We have important things to discuss."

Kanvar returned to the dinner chamber sometime later, his armor and face clean. Dharanidhar accompanied him. They were the last to arrive, and seven seats at the table were already taken. The vast space in the rest of the chamber was filled by six other dragons who stood behind their Nagas. Kumar Raza was the only person there who did not have a dragon. Tana, Denali, and Aadi were not present, nor Kanvar's mother, Mani, or Eska, Denali's mother. The meeting, it seemed, was just for fully bonded Nagas, with Kumar Raza being the only exception.

As Kanvar stepped into the room, everyone rose to their feet and Rajahansa growled, *You're late.*

"What? I'm not late. I was the first one here, but since no one else was here, I figured I'd go take a nap or something." Stupid gold dragon took everything too seriously.

"Kanvar," his father cautioned. He was dressed in shimmering gold finery even more gaudy than the table setting and chandelier.

Kanvar took a deep breath and limped over to the vacant seat. "Forgive me," Kanvar said, forcing his voice to sound sorry. "I did not mean to keep everyone waiting. Good evening, Karishi, welcome to the gilded birdcage."

Kanvar had never met Karishi in person before and had only experienced brief mental contact with him through Raahi's mind. He found Karishi to be an impressive man with the broad shoulders and bulging muscles of a master blacksmith. He wore copper dragonscale armor that moved with him as if it were his own hide. His face looked neither old nor young, and Kanvar couldn't put an age to it.

Karishi smiled. "Devaj said you had somewhat of an insolent attitude. I see he wasn't exaggerating."

"Kanvar," his father said. "I was just introducing Karishi to everyone present. If you'll just let me finish."

"Certainly." Kanvar bowed to his father. "I'm sorry for the interruption." Kanvar already knew everyone present. There weren't that many Nagas in the world. Just Parmver and his two sons, Haidar and Liander. Kanvar's father, Amar. Then Devaj and Kanvar, and finally Karishi.

Amar went on to introduce Haidar and Liander as the men who had designed and built the golden palace. Both of them were even older than Kanvar's father who was over five hundred years old.

"But no Naga women?" Karishi said, disappointed.

Amar shook his head. "My mother, Parmver's daughter, was the last female Naga that we know of. In truth, we will never know how many Nagas have been born but killed quietly by their families. Male or female, we have no count. But, today there is cause for celebration. Kanvar has discovered a girl who is almost certainly a Naga. I expect the fever will come upon her soon." His wide smile and sparkling eyes revealed how utterly pleased he was with Kanvar's discovery.

"Speaking of Tana, where is she?" Kanvar asked. "Is she all right? I need to talk to her. I don't want her to be angry with me."

"She's fine," Amar said. "The women are getting her settled in."

"Don't worry, Karishi," Parmver reached over and patted Karishi's arm. "There is plenty of opportunity for female companionship if that is what you were hoping for by coming here. There is a village hidden in the jungle where Naga blood runs deep. They do not hate or fear us.

We have all found wives there." His eyes flashed to Devaj and Kanvar. "All of us old enough to have married."

Kanvar's cheeks grew hot, and he hoped his face was not as red as Karishi's. Behind Karishi, Tazeran lashed his tail back and forth and started licking the floor. The gold leafing that covered everything in the palace melted on his tongue like sweet chocolate.

"Um." Kanvar raised his hand and pointed at Tazeran.

Karishi whipped around and threw his hands up in exasperation. "Tazeran, I told you, stop eating the palace. They'll send us back to Darvat and never let us return."

Tazeran raised his head with a guilty look on his face and licked the melted gold from his lips.

Dharanidhar filled the chamber with a bellowing laugh. *Eat up, little serpent. I won't stop you.*

"But if you're here, who is guarding the Hall?" Kanvar asked Karishi.

"Taz and I sealed it off completely, front and back. And we left Raahi to guard it. I think it will be safe enough." Karishi looked around at the gathered Naga. "If you'll let us, Tazeran and I would like to stay. It's just," he glanced at Taz, "Perhaps the palace isn't the best place for us. Is there a mountain close to this village?"

"Yes, in fact, there is," Amar said. "The village is built right up next to it. You can stay with the humans and Tazeran can devour whatever rock he likes. And speaking of food, I think since we're all here now, we should begin." He called out to Bellori with his mind.

A few moments later, Bellori and some of his fellow young gold dragons carried trays of food into the room and set them on the table. Roasted bovinder, steaming soups and pies, cooked vegetables, and a rainbow array of jungle fruits.

Amar sat and filled his plate, motioning for the others to help themselves as well.

Bellori poured sweet nectar into everyone's goblets then left, returning with large trays of steaming meats for the dragons present.

Kanvar filled his plate and then his mouth. He was famished after his battle with the volcanic dragon.

*Good thing I learned to stomach cooked food,* Dharanidhar said to Kanvar.

*You like it, and you know it. Don't think I haven't noticed you've got Bellori bringing all your meals to you cooked now.*

*Yes, well, it's not so bad when you get used to it.*

Kanvar's conversation with Dhar was interrupted as Amar got everyone's attention and started speaking again.

"I know you are all enjoying your meal, but we must discuss an important matter. Karishi has brought word to us that the singing stones house the spirits of our ancestors, and those spirits live in torment now that they have been removed from the walls of Stonefountain. He feels that we are duty bound to retrieve the stones and return them to the fountain so the spirits can rest in peace."

The table fell silent.

#Dragonbound IV

Kumar Raza raked his fingers through his beard. "Easier said than done. There are thousands of them, most held by dragon hunters or in the storerooms of powerful families. If any of you leave this palace and go out in the world searching for them, you'll be recognized as Nagas and killed. Such a quest could mean the final destruction of all Nagas."

Karishi jumped to his feet. "But we can't just leave them in agony. Have you no compassion?"

Amar lifted his hand. "Be still, Karishi. If I did not care, I would not have brought the subject up. I think in the very least we should test the idea. Kumar, you have a singing stone, yes?"

Kumar nodded.

"Would you be willing to sacrifice it for this cause?"

Kumar hesitated. "Singing stones are very valuable."

"Would you keep a living person in torment and slavery?" Karishi said. "No. Why would you even think to do it to one who is dead?"

Kanvar put his fork down on the table and cleared his throat. "I think what grandfather means is not that the stone is worth a lot of money, but that it is important for relationships between Nagas and humans. Without it, my mother could never be sure that she really loved my father. If she could not hold the stone and know for certain no Naga was controlling her, then she would have to assume her feelings of love were forced upon her by my father.

48

The singing stones create a balance between humans and Nagas that is our only hope of coexisting."

"No one here wants to coexist with humans," Haidar said. "We want to stay hidden from the world and live out our lives in peace."

"But it doesn't have to be that way," Kanvar said. Sweat trickled down his neck and beaded on his forehead. He was the youngest of the Nagas and half afraid to speak his mind in the face of his elders, but that didn't stop him. "Things can change. I know they can. Dhar and I are proof. Even Akshara acknowledged such a change before he died. If he, who once ordered the inhalation of all Nagas, could accept that there may be a place for us in the world then certainly we should not give up hope of that ever happening."

"At the expense of slavery and torment of how many souls?" Karishi slammed his fist on the table. "Torment Akshara condemned them to when he tore them from the walls of Stonefountain."

*Silence.* Rajahansa's command echoed through the minds of everyone present. *Kumar, you will take your stone to Stonefountain and put it into the water. Devaj will go with you so he can witness first hand whether or not the crystal really does house the spirit of the dead. We have not yet proved that Stonefountain really is like the Hall of Ancestors in Darvat. Until we know for sure one way or the other, this argument is meaningless.*

Karishi fell silent and Tazeran slithered under the table where Rajahansa couldn't see him and wrapped himself around Karishi's feet.

"Of course, I will do as you wish," Kumar Raza said. Though he was not a full Naga, the Naga blood that flowed through him allowed him to get the impression of what Rajahansa had just said, even though he could not hear the exact words.

Kanvar rose, no longer hungry and not wanting to spend another moment with the other Nagas. Dharanidhar remained quiet, but very aware that he and Kanvar were only guests here. They would never fit in.

*Come on Dhar*, Kanvar said as he limped toward the exit. *I think we've overstayed our welcome here.*

"Kanvar, wait," Devaj said. He left his place at the table and put an arm around his brother. "We do need to hear your opinions. That's why we wanted you here."

Kanvar shook his head. "Dhar and I don't belong."

"I disagree, but stay for just another moment. Karishi has something for you."

Kanvar turned back.

Karishi rose and held out a sealed parchment. "It's from General Chandran. Raahi gave it to me to deliver to you."

"What does it say?" Kanvar took the paper and noted that Chandran's seal remained unbroken.

Karishi shrugged. "It's for you. I didn't read it."

Kanvar broke the seal, unfolded the parchment, and read through Chandran's brief message. His heart skipped a beat.

"Is it something you want to share with the rest of us?" Amar asked.

Kanvar swallowed hard and laid the parchment on the table. "He says there is something strange happening with the Maran Senate. He wants me to come to the Maran outpost on the Second Finger to talk to him."

"It's a trap." Haidar jumped to his feet. "It has to be. Amar, you can't let him go."

Amar frowned. "It is unfortunate that Raahi told Chandran you are a Naga. We can't risk you going to talk to him."

Kanvar balled his hand into a fist. "Chandran is my friend. He was…more of a father to me than you ever were, and you do not tell me where I can and can't go. This might be our best chance to make peace with the other humans."

"Listen to me, Kanvar." Parmver hobbled over to him. "You can't make peace with them. Nothing good can come from such a meeting."

Kanvar growled under his breath and backed up into Dharanidhar's claw. Dharanidhar picked him up and bared his teeth at the other dragons. No one moved as Dhar carried Kanvar out of the chamber to the closest window overlooking the jungle and launched into the sky.

## Chapter Four

**Kumar Raza frowned as** Kanvar and his dragon left the chamber. "Amar, we can't let them go alone," he said to the king, his longtime friend, and son-in-law.

"We can't let them go at all," Haidar said, red faced. "If he gives away the location of this palace, we're dead. All of us."

Even not being a full Naga, Kumar could feel the fear rolling off him.

Amar spread his hands. "I can't force him to stay."

"Yes you can," Liander said, agreeing with his brother.

"No, not unless I want to become like King Khalid, and I refuse to abuse my power like that." Amar's voice was firm but gentle.

"You call keeping us safe abusing your power?"

"Yes, I do."

Kumar shook his head in annoyance as the Nagas fell to arguing amongst themselves about a moral code they should all agree to live by. "Well, I'm going after him, just in case it's a trap," Kumar said. "Kanvar may trust Chandran, but I don't trust the rest of the Maranies. Come on Devaj. We'll stop at Stonefountain on the way."

Kumar strode from the room and left the bickering Nagas behind.

Devaj hurried after him. "I don't think Kanvar would act so defiant if he weren't bound to that blue dragon. Dharanidhar has twisted his mind, and it's my fault. He did it to save me. Now he'll suffer the rest of his life for it."

Kumar entered his personal chambers. Miki, his gray and white sled dog, let out a happy bark and jumped up, putting his front feet on Kumar's chest and licking his face. Kumar rubbed him behind the ears then pushed him away. "Devaj, we don't know if Dharanidhar has twisted Kanvar's personality or merely fit what was already there."

Miki went back to chewing an old bone he had snatched from the kitchen.

"He's my brother. I know. Kanvar was never like that before," Devaj said.

"He's my grandson, and I know as well. He was always headstrong and determined" Kumar Raza donned his armor as he spoke.

"Not like this. I was just talking to him, and he slugged me in the gut. Bensharie saved his life, and Kanvar yelled at him for it. Grandfather, that blue dragon has changed him.

He should have bonded to a gold. They're far more human. They think like us, they live like us, they have the same cultural structure and morals."

"Devaj." Kumar put a firm hand on his grandson's shoulder. "I don't think Dharanidhar has changed him as much as you presume. Life changed Kanvar. He was only a child when you and his father abandoned him to be killed. Alone, crippled, desperate, he managed to survive. No one could go through that without becoming bitter and defiant. Violent even. He's had to fight to stay alive. That is not Dharanidhar's fault. If anything, I think the old blue dragon tempers Kanvar's mood swings."

Kumar buckled on his weapons and supplies and retrieved the little iron box containing his dragonstone from its place at the bottom of his chest. "Do you wish to pack anything, Devaj, or do you plan to go as you are? We need to hurry so he doesn't get too far ahead of us."

Devaj ran his fingers through his golden hair and looked around as if unsure what he should take.

"Warm robes. It gets cold over the ocean. Water to drink. Food to eat unless you're fine with sharing anything I hunt down. But I know you aren't fond of meat. Oh, and your father's sword. Go get it from him. We may need it." Kumar checked his own sword, his crossbow, bolts, and hunting knife. They all looked clean and sharp, but then he took special care each day to maintain them. When Devaj still stood flustered and unmoving, Kumar grabbed a full waterskin and pouch of travel rations—hard bread, cheese, and jerky—things he always kept filled and ready just in case. He was a dragon hunter after all.

"I don't want to fight the Maranies," Devaj said. Last time he'd gone to find Kanvar he'd almost been burned at the stake.

"With any luck, we won't have to. Here." Kumar tossed Devaj a warm cloak. "Tell your father to meet us in the entry hall with his sword." Rolling his shoulders to loosen his stiff muscles, Kumar stepped outside of his chambers. "Where's Eska and Denali?" he asked Devaj.

Devaj, distracted by a mental conversation with his father, didn't answer for a moment.

Kumar raked his fingers through his beard and forced himself to wait patiently. When Devaj stopped staring off into space, he again asked after his wife and son.

"They're with Mani and Kanvar's girlfriend from the village."

"What chamber. I need to tell them I'm leaving."

"Oh, just down the hall there." Devaj pointed to a door set back away from Kumar's chambers.

"I'll meet you and Elkatran at the entrance hall."

Devaj nodded and walked back toward the meeting chamber.

Kumar Raza found Eska and Mani fawning over a young girl from the village. The girl looked nervous, but they were doing their best to make her feel at home.

"Father, you're back." Denali raced across the room and hugged him.

"No. Not really." He patted Denali on the back and brushed a kiss across Eska's lips. "I'm sorry. I have to go to Darvat again. I promise when I get back I'll spend a good deal of time with you and Denali."

Eska grabbed his beard and forced his face back down to hers for a proper kiss, one that made Kumar very sorry he had to leave her.

"I'll come back soon, I promise," he said when she was done.

She smiled and waved him away. "Go. Hunt. Enjoy yourself."

Kumar grimaced and gave Denali's arm a squeeze. "Look after your mother for me."

"I will."

Kumar hesitated. He had missed Eska and Denali while he was away. But thoughts of Kanvar facing the Maran general alone and the odds of it being a trap, got him moving. He strode to the entrance hall, anxious to be on his way.

Carrying Kanvar, Dharanidhar glided into the cave at the top of the cliff where they made their home. It was nothing like the golden palace, just jagged rock walls and a dirt floor, strewn with pebbles. Kanvar had a bedroll there, an extra change of clothes, a pot for cooking, and a wooden bowl and spoon. A campfire was his only light source. He unbuckled his flight harness and let Dharanidhar set him down.

Dharanidhar folded his wings and made himself comfortable in the depression in the center of the cave. *It's late in the afternoon to be starting a flight across the ocean.*

"I know." Kanvar limped over to the other chests Akshara had carved. The old dragon had collected and fashioned some interesting objects over the years, and Kanvar had not yet taken the time to look through them all. But he knew the thing he needed was right at the top. He opened the lid of one of the chests and pulled out the iron box that lay there.

The last time he'd seen Akshara's singing stone, it had been on a chain draped around Devaj's neck. It was the biggest singing stone Kanvar had ever encountered, and the iron box was large enough to hold the stone and the chain it was attached to. Kanvar shuddered as he picked it up. But he'd promised Chandran that if he would meet him, then he would bring Akshara's stone to protect Chandran's mind. The box fit snugly into the large leather pouch attached to his belt.

*We should sleep here tonight,* Dharanidhar said. *Think this through. Plan and pack and leave in the morning. Trouble with the Maran Senate does not constitute an emergency, and I don't think your father will follow us up here to try and stop us.*

Kanvar's body ached from his adventure with Tana in the jungle, but he was too tense to rest. "Let me just grab a couple of things. There's enough daylight left to at least fly down to the coast."

Dharanidhar shook himself, and several old scales clattered to the ground. *You think if we stay, Anilon will challenge me for leadership of the pride?*

*I might.* Anilon flapped into the cave and settled onto his hind legs. His wings remained outstretched in a show of defiance. *You've been gone a lot, Dharanidhar. Spending months at a time with the Nagas at the palace. Most of the pride thinks you are no longer fit to lead us. It is my duty to take you down.*

Kanvar snatched his crossbow free from its harness and loaded it while his heart did a double flip. Anilon was Dharanidhar's closest friend in the pride. If he felt he must challenge Dhar, than the whole pride must have turned against him.

Dharanidhar let out a low chuckle and made no move to match Anilon's aggressive display. His personal shields slipped a little and Kanvar became aware of the constant ache Dhar had been feeling in his legs and wing. His flight into the hurricane had cost him more than Kanvar had realized. Dhar had hidden it, but though his bones had mended, the pain had not left him.

Kanvar gasped and fell to his knees.

Dharanidhar snapped his shield back up tight between Kanvar and the pain.

*Anilon, my friend.* Dharanidhar bowed to the other dragon. *I concede leadership of the pride to you. I am hurt beyond healing. Kanvar and I have only returned to collect our things, then we will be gone into permanent exile.*

Kanvar climbed to his feet, put his crossbow away, and scrubbed tears from his eyes. He needed to be able to see for both of them.

Anilon lowered his wings and dropped to all fours. *You're hurt? What happened?*

Dharanidhar shook his head. *An accident. That's all. I am old. The pride needs a new leader. Can you hold the position, or should I take someone down for you before I leave? Omarion, perhaps. He thinks he has learned to fight well enough to make a try for it.*

*I can handle Omarion.*

*Then I leave Akshara's things to you, all that which Kanvar hasn't already claimed.* Dharanidhar bowed once more to Anilon to show his submission.

Anilon let out a deep purring sound from the back of his throat and rubbed his head against Dharanidhar's neck. *I will miss you, Dhar. You taught me to fight and kept me alive when I was small, awkward, and easy game for the larger dragons my age. You've done more for this pride than any dragon since Akshara. I do not like to see you go like this.*

*You'd rather kill me in a fight?*

*It would be more honorable for you. A bright end to an illustrious life.*

Dharanidhar snorted. *I agree, Anilon, and I would do it that way if I were not bound to Kanvar. He's barely more than a child. I cannot snuff his life out so soon. I must go on living, whatever the disgrace.*

*He dies if you do?* Anilon said in surprise.

*Yes, of course. Our lives are bound together now.*

Kanvar gritted his teeth, threw his extra clothes onto his bedding, and rolled it up along with his cooking and eating supplies. The rest of his belongings he carried on his person or had left back at the palace. He did not like to think that he could be the cause of any disgrace for Dharanidhar.

"I will fight to the death with you, Dhar," Kanvar blurted out. "You know that. It's my fault you are hurt. If it has to be that way, let us go down fighting."

Dhar lifted Kanvar up onto his neck. *No, Kanvar. We will go on living. It would be a greater disgrace to throw your life away so casually.*

Dharanidhar grabbed the chest where he kept his own things. There wasn't much in it that he really cared about, a few mementos of his lost mate and hatchlings. And the shiny gold coins he'd collected during his war with the Maranies. The money didn't matter to him, but he knew Kanvar needed it. Then he launched himself into the sky. *We will go to the coast like you suggested.*

*I don't like it,* Devaj said to Elkatran as they flew over the Varnan savanna south of Daro. He scanned the horizon for signs of Kanvar and Dharanidhar like he had since they'd left the golden palace the day before, never seeing a flash of blue or encountering Kanvar's consciousness with his mind.

*Dharanidhar's bigger than I am,* Elkatran answered. *Maybe he's that much faster too. It did take a few minutes for us to get off after them. Perhaps we shouldn't have slept for the night when we reached the Varnan coast.*

Kumar Raza shifted restlessly. He sat behind Devaj on Elkatran's neck. "We'll be to Stonefountain soon. Do we fly on and keep searching, or stop and do what his Majesty ordered?"

"I don't know." Devaj rolled his stiff shoulders. Though the sun was hot, the wind chilled him. The taste of desert dust clung to his lips. A small part of him was excited to see Stonefountain, but for the most part he did not relish the idea. It was one thing reading about the atrocities that went on there, it was another seeing it in person.

"Can you sense Kanvar yet? Surely you should be able to pick up his thoughts," Kumar Raza said.

"I told you, I tried. He's shielding them. I may be older than Kanvar, but Dharanidhar is ancient and power-ful. I doubt even my father and Rajahansa could penetrate his shields if he was serious about stopping them." Devaj gritted his teeth. Every time he thought about his little brother bonding with that monster just to save him, it made his heart twist in a knot. If there was any way he could free his brother from Dharanidhar, he would. He'd searched in all the books back at the palace for an answer, some way to break the bond. But it seemed the only way to do it would be to kill Dharanidhar, which would kill Kanvar as well.

*Let it go*, Elkatran said. *Kanvar seems happy with his choice, and Parmver told you he's certain Dharanidhar is not abusing him in any way.*

*I don't care what Parmver says.*

Their argument cut off as the rubble-strewn slopes of Stonefountain came into view. Crumbling buildings, falling away to dust, stones toppled, towers fallen, and utter desolation over the expanse of what was once a vast city. The water that tumbled down from the palace on the mountain overlooking the city slugged along in a muddy brown wash. The grass that grew abundantly on the savanna, thinned the closer it came to the riverbanks.

A heavy weight settled onto Devaj's shoulders, and he shuddered. "Nothing grows by the river, Raza. Why is that? Where there is water, shouldn't there be life?"

"I noticed that last time I was here, but couldn't see why. The Darvaties call the river that spawns from the Hall of their Ancestors the River of Death, but trees and plants grow all along its banks."

"That's not reassuring," Devaj said. "I don't want to be here. I don't want to do this. And I'm worried about Kanvar."

Elkatran rumbled in agreement, but flapped toward the mountain anyway. The crumbling houses grew bigger as they climbed the slopes. The remains of the palace were massive, but arched ceilings had fallen, leaving open chambers bare to sun, wind, and rain. Dark stains marred cracked marble floors that had once been covered in gold—the blood of his slaughtered ancestors, the flesh and bones of the bodies picked clean and scattered by spine-back raptors long ago.

Elkatran growled. *You have too much of an imagination. These are nothing but empty buildings. Don't conjure ghosts to inhabit them.* He landed near the top of the mountain, in a chamber from which the water gushed forth through a conduit from deep inside. The ceiling and walls had fallen into mounds of rubble, but an opening had been cleared by dragon hunters in search of singing stones, revealing a hall that led into the mountain.

Devaj dismounted and slid to the ground. "You have your stone, Grandfather?" A fretful wind tangled his hair.

Kumar Raza dropped to the ground beside him. "It would be a waste of time coming here if I didn't." His muscled frame, blood-red armor, and weapons strapped to his back, should have made Devaj feel safe, but a sudden fright took him, and he edged back behind Elkatran. Kumar Raza was a dragon hunter, and dragon hunters killed Nagas. And he had a singing stone.

*Be at peace,* Elkatran said. *If he tries anything, I'll blast him with my joy breath.*

Devaj shook himself. *You won't fit into that passage. I have to go in there alone with him.*

"What's wrong?" Kumar Raza said.

"I don't like this place." Devaj rubbed his hand down Elkatran's smooth plates, drawing courage from his companion.

"Of course you don't, and you won't like it even more when we get inside the chamber with the fountain. Kanvar only went in for a moment, and I swear it nearly killed him. Karishi's crazy to think the Nagas can do this. It's like walking into the very heart of a thousand singing stones."

Devaj leaned his forehead against Elkatran's side. He had to do this; Rajahansa had ordered it.

"I can take the stone and dump it in the fountain myself," Kumar Raza said. "You can stay here if you want."

"No." Devaj pulled away, squared his shoulders, and marched toward the opening. "You wouldn't be able to see the spirit leave the stone and settle into the fountain, if there is one. I have to be there to find the answers we need."

"You won't be able to feel Elkatran once you go in there."

"I've dealt with singing stones before. Believe me, I know what it feels like." Devaj shook aside his fear. "Let's just get this done with." He passed into the hall but found it rough going over the fallen rubble that choked the passageway. "How did Kanvar even get through this?" he muttered.

"With difficulty." Kumar Raza came along behind Devaj. "In fact, for the first time in his life I believe he actually asked Raahi for help."

Devaj chuckled, wishing he could have been with Kanvar all those years that he had spent indentured to Chandran. He envied Raahi's relationship with Kanvar. It was frustrating knowing that Kanvar had been there in Kundiland for so long, so close, and Devaj and his father had not known. So much time they should have had together as a family wasted and gone. And Kanvar changed because of it, his mind taken over by the blue dragon, never again to be the charming little brother Devaj had adored.

Devaj climbed over a large mound of rubble and stopped to catch his breath on the other side. He wiped dust and sweat from his face and licked his lips.

Kumar Raza jumped down beside him and leaned against the wall. "You should exercise more, Devaj. You've grown soft for the son of a dragon hunter."

"My father is not a dragon hunter. He's a king. He never would have killed anything if you hadn't made him."

"I had no choice. He wanted to marry your mother. The dragon hunter jati would have suspected he was a Naga right away if he—"

The wall crumbled and Kumar Raza fell backwards, vanishing into a sunken chamber beyond.

## Chapter Five

**"Grandfather?" Devaj called** through the cloud of dust kicked up by the falling stones.

"I'm all right," Kumar Raza called up from below. "Just bruised a bit. But it's dark down here. I'm going to need some light to climb back up."

A blue light appeared from down in the hole, and the wail of Kumar Raza's singing stone stung Devaj's mind. He tried to block out the sound, but couldn't do it even at that distance.

"Amazing," Raza's voice drifted up to him faintly through the piercing song of the stone. "Devaj, you should come down here. Parmver's going to love this."

Steeling himself, Devaj knelt down and leaned through the breach in the wall.

Kumar Raza stood on a gold-covered floor six feet below. His singing stone lit the untouched chamber with a pale blue light, illuminating shelf after shelf of books, stretching off into the darkness. Books etched into clay tablets, scrolls of vellum and papyrus, paper books bound in leather.

"It's as big as the Chronicler Jati Repository in Daro. Bigger maybe." Kumar Raza's voice floated up to Devaj and vanished into the dark expanses of the chamber outside of the stone's light.

Sweat soaked Devaj's robes, and his eyes stung. The gold dragons at the palace would fly cartwheels at the thought of seeing this. He tried to project an image of it to Elkatran, but the singing stone blocked his power. "How many of those books do you think we could carry?" he called down to Kumar Raza.

"Not a thousandth of what I bet you're wishing we could." Raza pulled a vellum scroll from a canister on the closest shelf and eased it open.

"What does it say?"

Kumar Raza positioned the stone so he could read it. "It's a map."

"A map? Just a map? Try another one."

Kumar Raza rolled up the map, stuck it under his arm, and reached for another scroll.

A rumble sounded above Devaj's head, and loose pebbles and sand showered down on him.

Kumar Raza's gaze snapped up at the sound. "Get out of here, Devaj," he shouted, "before that whole hall comes down on top of you."

"I'm not leaving without you. Come on. Can you climb up here?" He motioned for his grandfather to climb up the pile of stones that had fallen into the room with him.

Kumar Raza glanced back at all the endless shelves of books. He grabbed every scroll he could carry in one arm and started his climb back up to Devaj.

The floor rumbled and swayed beneath Devaj's knees. He motioned for Kumar Raza to hurry. Raza tossed the singing stone up beside Devaj and used his free hand to help him climb the last few feet. Ignoring the pain of the stone, Devaj grabbed his arm as it emerged at the top and hauled his grandfather up.

The ceiling groaned again, and more sand trickled down into their faces. The floor buckled.

"Come on." Kumar Raza snatched up the singing stone and ran down the hall toward the fountain.

Devaj followed.

Behind them the floor slumped off into the chamber below. Then the walls buckled and the ceiling came down in a thundering crash of heavy stone, cutting off their way back.

Devaj paused to look behind him at the destruction, but Kumar Raza grabbed him and forced him to keep moving until they'd climbed over a big mound of rubble, slipped through a thin opening, and came down on the other side into a natural mountain chamber.

The wail of thousands of tormented voices in a shattered song tore at Devaj's mind. He gasped and pressed his hands to his head. A fountain welled up at the center of the chamber and gathered in a stone basin, overflowing into a rush of water that raced down into a dark conduit to come out in the hall where Elkatran had landed them. The fountain glowed with light and power, illuminating the walls that had once been lined with crystals. The few remaining crystals that stuck out between jagged empty gashes glowed as well, spreading through the room in a pastel rainbow.

Devaj found himself unable to move or speak in the face of the blinding song, but Kumar Raza wrapped a strong arm around his shoulders and guided him over to the basin. He pressed his own singing stone into Devaj's hand and motioned to the water.

Devaj dropped to his knees. The blue stone pulsed in his hand, but its voice was lost in the screams of the stones on the walls around him.

Tears streaming from his eyes, Devaj lowered his hand with the singing stone into the water. The light pulsed once, then flowed from the stone into the fountain. It shimmered into the form of a face from some man that had lived in the ancient past. But the spirit, instead of being at peace, looked up at Devaj with agony-filled eyes. The man screamed and kept screaming as his spirit spread out and joined the others in the hall.

Devaj let the stone slip through his fingers to the bottom of the pool, but when he tried to pull his hand from the water, some force grabbed it and held him in place. The water shimmered, and another spirit appeared.

Ancient and terrifying, it seemed to possess all the power of Stonefountain and control the living essence of every spirit trapped in the place. A face coalesced in the water and looked up at Devaj. It was twisted in eternal torment and hatred, but Devaj recognized it from pictures in books and paintings he'd seen.

King Khalid, the tyrant of Stonefountain, looked up at Devaj and howled.

Devaj fought to pull his hand away, but Khalid's mind tore into his, shattering shields, delving into every tender spot and personal memory, binding Devaj's mind with steel cords. *I have waited long for a new body to inhabit. Come, Little Prince, it is your honor to free me from this prison of agony.*

Devaj tried to scream as Khalid's spirit sliced like hot iron through his own, but Khalid would not let him make a sound.

Devaj's mind exploded in pain as some outside force jerked his hand out of the water. King Khalid's hold on him slipped away as Kumar Raza flung him over his shoulder, raced across the chamber to where the water swirled into the conduit, and dived in. Devaj gasped, and icy water filled his mouth and nose. He tried to cough it out, but more rushed in. Blackness surrounded him as the current dragged him through its course surrounded by heavy stone until it thrust him out in the chamber where he'd left Elkatran. But the force of the river pushed him and Kumar Raza passed the startled dragon and shot them off the edge of the chamber to fall in a frothing white waterfall down the mountain.

As soon as Devaj cleared the chamber, Elkatran's thoughts snapped into his terrorized mind. Elkatran launched himself in the air and swooped down to catch Devaj and Kumar Raza.

*What happened?* Elkatran asked as he flew to the base of the falls and set them on the riverbank.

But Devaj was in too much pain, shock, and terror to say anything besides. "Khalid. Khalid. Khalid." His body shook out of control. His mind felt like it had been shredded by dragon claws.

Kanvar stroked Dharanidhar's neck as the sun slipped down behind them. Ahead of them, the mountain of Stonefountain rose on the horizon. Dharanidhar glided across the savanna, letting the hot air currents rising from the ground keep him aloft, only flapping now and again to adjust his course. They'd spent the previous night on the Kundiland coast in the cove where the Great Blue dragons used to nest. Dharanidhar had spoken little, thinking about how his mate and hatchlings had been killed in that spot. Kanvar knew there was nothing he could say that would ease the pain of the past or the sting of Dharanidhar's present exile from the pride.

In the morning, they'd left Dharanidhar's things in his old lair and started across the ocean, flying slow and easy. When they reached the Varnan coast, they'd landed and Dhar napped before taking off again. Kanvar worried about his aching bones and joints, but Dharanidhar kept them shielded from him. The best Kanvar could do for his friend was insist that they land and rest often.

*We should stop here for the night,* Kanvar suggested. *We can skirt around Stonefountain in the morning. I don't want to go anywhere near it.*

Dharanidhar rumbled in agreement, but a shock of pain and terror sliced through Kanvar's mind. "That's Devaj," he shouted. "He's hurt, Dhar. Up ahead, at Stonefountain."

Dharanidhar pumped his wings, and they shot across the grasslands toward the mountain ahead.

*Devaj?* Kanvar tried to connect with his brother's mind, but it was a shredded chaos of fear and pain. *Elkatran, where are you?* If Devaj was at Stonefountain, his dragon had to be there with him.

*Here, Kanvar.* Elkatran's mind met his own. It was filled with worry for Devaj, but Elkatran had thrown up a shield between himself and his Naga to keep his own mind clear.

*What happened?* Kanvar asked.

*I don't know. Something inside the chamber. Our minds were separated by the singing stones. Raza says Devaj put the stone into the water and then went rigid and started to shake. Raza dragged him out of there, but Devaj has been hurt badly. It must have been the voice of the singing stones. But for some reason he keeps calling for King Khalid.*

Dharanidhar followed Elkatran's thoughts to the riverbank below the waterfall. He landed and lifted Kanvar to the ground. Kanvar limped over to where his brother lay shaking in the dust. His face was as white as bleached bones. His eyes stared up into the sky, seeing nothing. He muttered Khalid's name over and over again under his breath.

Kumar Raza knelt beside him, holding him in place so he wouldn't hurt himself with his thrashing. Raza glanced up as Kanvar approached. "Rajahansa should never have let Karishi convince him to do this."

Kanvar knelt on the opposite side of his brother and eased his palm down across Devaj's forehead, steeling his own mind against his brother's pain and confusion. He sensed that some powerful Naga had raked through Devaj's thoughts, plundered his memories, and tried to trap and control his mind. The force and extent of the devastation was appalling.

Fighting back a headache, Kanvar eased his hand away. "How long was he in the fountain chamber?"

"One minute. Maybe two. I got him out of there as fast as I could."

Kanvar shook his head.

"Khalid!" Devaj screamed then fell unconscious.

Kanvar grimaced. What Naga could have done so much damage to another Naga so quickly? Surely Devaj knew how to shield his mind. But then how could he with so many singing stones around him? The stones blocked all Naga powers, Devaj's mind should have been safe.

"Was there anyone else in the chamber?" he asked Kumar Raza.

Raza shook his head. "Just the two of us."

Kanvar gazed up toward the top of the waterfall, trying to think what might have happened. A finger of cold slid down his spine. Karishi had been bound with General Samdrasen's singing stone when he'd contacted Raahi's mind from the other side of the world. Not the singing stone, nor the distance, nor the fact that Raahi was not a Naga had broken their communication, because he was connected to the stones in the chamber, to the spirits of his ancestors.

"Khalid." Kanvar jumped to his feet. "King Khalid." Who else could be so powerful, could do so much damage so quickly? "We need to get out of here." But could any distance separate Devaj's mind from the spirits of the dead once they'd been joined?

Dharanidhar let out a ferocious roar and lit the darkening sky with blue fire.

Kumar Raza grabbed Kanvar's arm. "What's going on?"

"Devaj must have been attacked by King Khalid's spirit. It tried to take over his mind. The damage is extensive. You and Elkatran have to get him back to Parmver and my father quickly. Tell them to build the strongest shield they can to protect Devaj's mind from future incursion. Elkatran, can you fly at night?"

Elkatran ruffled his wings in agitation. *I can fly.*

"Good. Grandfather, you'll have to sit behind Devaj and hold him in place."

Kumar Raza frowned and looked from west to east, from the way they'd come to the direction of Darvat. "You should come back with us, Kanvar. This is serious. Your father will want you there."

Kanvar tensed. Chandran waited for him on the Second Finger. "There's nothing I could do back at the palace. I know nothing about healing the kind of hurt Devaj has taken. And I think it's important that I meet with Chandran."

Kumar Raza took a firm hold of Kanvar's shoulders and looked him straight in the eyes. "Kanvar, listen to me. This meeting is a trap. The Maranies know what you are, and they want to kill you. Chandran may have good intentions. I believe you when you say he would not hurt you, but he's not alone. I was supposed to follow you and make sure none of the other Maranies attack while you're meeting with him. But if I have to take Devaj back, you must come with me. You cannot rush into this alone. Please, come to the palace, and then you and I can go together to meet with Chandran."

Kanvar looked from his injured brother to Dharanidhar. The grizzled blue dragon, covered with scars, blind, his body hurting. If he and Dhar flew back to the golden palace now, chances were Dhar would curl up and never move far again. Kanvar knew he should want Dharanidhar to be comfortable and happy. Safe. Well fed.

Dharanidhar let out a shattering roar. He blew out another spurt of intense blue fire, snatched Kanvar up in his claw, and launched into the air, flapping furiously eastward. *You and I will go down fighting gloriously yet,* he said to Kanvar.

# Chapter Six

**Two days later,** the string of islands off the southern tip of Darvat came into view on the horizon. After leaving Devaj and Kumar Raza behind, Kanvar and Dharanidhar had continued their slow journey across Varna and out to sea. They had spoken little, just flying, eating and resting, and flying again. Dharanidhar had fought the Maranies for long enough he did not doubt Kumar Raza's assertion that they were flying into a trap. Kanvar wanted to think otherwise.

The salty ocean wind whipped his hair as he squinted to see the black smudges on the horizon.

Dharanidhar dropped low to the water, skimming the tops of the waves. *They'll have spy glasses watching the sky for us and heavy ballista mounted on the walls of their outpost. They are expecting us. Thank Raahi for telling him that not only are you a Naga but you are bound to his biggest enemy.*

Kanvar couldn't figure how his best friend could have been so stupid, but he forgave Raahi. *How do we approach without them seeing us then?*

*That's the tricky part, but I have an idea.* Dharanidhar changed his course further eastward, so he could approach the string of islands from the back side opposite of the Maran outpost. He stayed low over the water, and when the Second Finger came within clear sight, he flared his wings and splashed down into the undulating waves.

Kanvar tensed, remembering the hurricane that had torn him from Dharanidhar's back and crushed Dharanidhar beneath the churning surface last time they'd flown above these waters. But this time, the day was bright and sunny and Dharanidhar did not sink. With his wings tucked at his sides, he floated easily on the water.

*Relax,* he told Kanvar. *The ocean front is my natural home. I can swim as easily as I can fly. Easier nowadays.*

Kanvar tried to relax, but his stomach churned at the constant rise and fall of the ocean waves as Dharanidhar swam toward the island. Water splashed up his legs and ran in rivulets down his blue dragonscale armor. When Dhar reached the beach, he stayed in the water, turning so he swam along the shoreline. The taste of brine clung to Kanvar's lips and tongue. He decided he preferred flying over swimming any day. But through this method they got within sight of the Maran outpost without the toll of the warning bell.

As soon as they were close enough Kanvar could walk to the outpost, Dhar climbed up on the beach and lumbered into the palm trees, forcing his way deep into the thicket of plant growth below the palms so that the leaves hid his body from sight.

He lowered Kanvar to the ground. *Be careful. Stay back and watch the outpost for a while. See what they're doing. Look for a trap. See if you can think of a way to meet with General Chandran alone. Do not let yourself be seen by anyone else.*

Kanvar peeked out of the trees toward the outpost. The wooden stockade was built close to the shore next to the mouth of the river. A tall fence of sharpened wooden spikes surrounded the barracks, stables, and buildings. There were platforms at each of the four corners for mounted ballistae, but three of the platforms were empty. On the fourth, a team of soldiers were at work lowering the ballistae to the ground outside the stockade. The main gates were flung open, and the full strength of the garrison seemed to be busy hauling out weapons and supplies and loading them on the large warship that sat anchored beside a dock.

*The outpost is all wooden*, Kanvar thought to Dharanidhar. *It wouldn't last a moment against blue dragons. But I suppose it wasn't built to fight the blues just the Darvaties. But why are the Maranies abandoning the outpost? Surely they need to have some men close to Darvat to get their cut of money from Darvati commerce.*

*Perhaps Chandran figured out I was coming*, Dharanidhar said.

79

*Of course he knows you're coming. He invited us here.* Kanvar inched along the tree line, drawing closer to the fort without being seen.

General Chandran strode out of the stockade, his blue dragonhide armor and gold general's braid glimmering in the sunlight. The frown on his face along with his gray hair made him seem older than Kanvar remembered him. He supervised the loading of the final ballistae and supplies then ordered his men up on the boat as well. While the last of the soldiers climbed up the gangplank, Chandran scanned the skies.

*He's looking for us*, Kanvar told Dharanidhar. With his good hand, he eased the iron box with Akshara's dragonstone from its pouch.

*As soon as you open that, we won't be able to communicate with each other*, Dharanidhar reminded him.

*I know.*

After the last soldier had boarded the boat, Chandran tore his gaze from the sky and shook his head.

Kanvar moved as close as he could to the outpost without being seen, but the Maranies had cleared the trees and plants well back from the walls so Kanvar couldn't get up close without coming out in the open.

"All aboard and ready, sir," the ship captain called down to General Chandran.

Chandran waved acknowledgement. "I'll be right up." Then he headed back toward the stockade.

Kanvar let out a whistling screech like the sound of a black monkey.

Chandran froze, knowing black monkeys only lived in the Kundiland jungles.

Kanvar set the iron box down in the sand, stepped back so he was well hidden in the trees, and screeched again.

*Be careful. Be ready to use your weapons to defend yourself,* Dharanidhar cautioned.

*Right.* Kanvar ran his hand along his crossbow strapped to his back and the hunting knife in its sheath at his waist but left them in place as Chandran turned and strode toward the trees.

Chandran didn't notice the iron box until he almost stepped on it. Then he picked it up and stared at it for a long moment before opening the lid and looking inside. He caught hold of the chain and lifted the glowing purple stone from the box.

Kanvar gasped as the piercing wail cut through his mind. It was hard to take, but he'd promised Chandran the safety of the stone if he ever wanted to meet with him.

Chandran's eyes snapped up in the direction of the sound. "Kanvar?" he called.

Kanvar glanced around to double check there were no other soldiers in the trees and he and Chandran were alone. When he was sure he was safe, he called out softly, "Step into the trees where the soldiers can't see you."

Chandran frowned and remained where he was.

"It's just me. Dharanidhar's not in here. You'd be able to see him if he was. And you have the stone, so you know I can't hurt you."

"You have a crossbow I'll wager."

"You have a sword. Besides, why would I come here to shoot you? You've been like a father to me." Sweat slicked Kanvar's palm, and the pain from the singing stone made him dizzy. "Come on Chandran. You asked me to come here. What do you want?"

Chandran dropped the stone back into the iron box and closed the lid. Then he strode into the trees toward the sound of Kanvar's voice.

The wail of the singing stone vanished for a moment, but a new one took its place as Chandran advanced. A single female voice, high and beautiful and filled with such torment it brought tears to Kanvar's eyes.

Chandran caught sight of Kanvar and stopped a couple of yards away. He held up the box. "I don't need your stone. I have my own." He caught hold of a silver chain around his neck and eased a pale white crystal from beneath his armor. "Beautiful isn't it?"

"Yes beautiful." Kanvar had never heard a song so beautiful and so terrible. It stabbed him to the core and made his legs buckle. He slumped to his knees, tears streaming down his cheeks.

"That's funny," Chandran said looking from his stone to the iron box that held Akshara's. "You'd think the bigger stone would be more powerful."

Kanvar brushed the water from his eyes and looked up at Chandran. "Akshara's stone works over a greater distance. Yours is just more…" Kanvar imagined a beautiful woman, delicate and regal, with pale skin and black hair. Her fingers cold as ice. Her smile beautiful and deadly.

"More what?"

"Feminine," Kanvar choked out.

"What?"

"The spirit in the stone. She's a woman. Powerful, ancient, irresistible, bathed in torment." Kanvar struggled back to his feet. "Why did you call me here, Chandran?"

Chandran's face twisted in an angry frown. "I'm sure you already know, Naga."

The sudden coldness in Chandran's voice made Kanvar shiver. "Your letter said there was something wrong in the Maran Senate. But I don't know what."

"Yes you do. And I'm ordering you to stop it. This is your only warning."

"Stop what? I don't know what you're talking about." A dark feeling crept over Kanvar. Something had turned Chandran even further against him.

Chandran let out a dry laugh. "You want to play innocent, but I'm not stupid. Suddenly, for no reason, the senate deposes the ruling Prime Minister in a unanimous vote. And replaces him unanimously with a twenty-one-year old farm boy from Longshire."

"So?" Kanvar was at a complete loss to understand what about that situation had Chandran so angry.

Chandran set the iron box in the sand, drew his sword, and pointed it at Kanvar. "Never in Maran history has the senate voted unanimously on anything. This is Naga work, Kanvar. I don't know what you hope to gain by taking control of the Maran government and ordering me to gather the full strength of our army and navy to the capital at Wareham, but I'm going back there now, and I will kill every last one of your Naga friends who are behind this."

"No. No, this is wrong." Kanvar spread his hand. "I talked to them just before coming here. They want nothing to do with any humans. All they want is to live their life in peace, away from everyone."

"Liar!" Chandran readied his sword to attack.

Kanvar stepped back and pulled out his hunting knife. "No. It's the truth. Chandran, believe me."

Chandran sneered. "Nothing you say can change the facts. A Naga has taken over the Maran Senate and made himself Prime Minister."

Kanvar struggled to think around the stabbing song of Chandran's stone. "If there's a Naga in the senate, it's no one I know, and none that I know would condone what you're saying he has done. Maybe you and I can work together to stop him."

"Nice thought. The problem is, I can't trust you, Kanvar."

"You trusted me enough to call me here. Or was your only intention to trap me and kill me like everyone insists?"

Kanvar inched back another step, readying to defend himself from Chandran's sword.

"My intention is to tell you to get out of Maran and stay out."

"Chandran, it can't be me. You know it can't be me. I can't hide my deformity. If the new Prime Minister were a cripple, everyone would be talking about it."

"You could be controlling this farm boy."

"Not if I'm here."

"Yes, if you're here. You need only plant the directions in his mind that will force him to carry out your will."

"Really? I didn't know that."

Chandran glared at him. "Don't think I haven't studied every last bit of information about Nagas since we spoke last. You have endless ways of controlling people."

Kanvar shook his head. "My training has been in moral conduct, how to control my powers to *not* hurt people or force them against their will. The Naga teaching me is strict and adamant about not repeating any of the evils done at Stonefountain."

Chandran advanced a step, sword threatening. "How many Nagas are there?"

Kanvar's heart raced. A bitter taste spread across his tongue, and he realized why Chandran had wanted to talk to him. Chandran was gathering information, trying to learn as much as he could about his enemy before making plans to attack and destroy. Kanvar backed up another step and came up against a palm tree.

"How many?" Chandran stepped forward and leveled his sword so that a single lunge would stab Kanvar through the heart.

Kanvar shook his head. "No one wants to fight you, General."

"Where are your vile friends staying? Here, with Karishi? But wait, Raahi tells me Karishi has gone...to Kundiland, he said. Is that where they are? Or is Raahi lying and it's really Karishi taking over the senate?"

Kanvar opened his mouth to argue that Karishi was safely out of the way in Kundiland, but he choked back his retort. It would confirm Raahi's claim that the Nagas lived in Kundiland and give Chandran a target.

"Karishi is not behind this take over of the Maran government," Kanvar said. He wished the singing stone would be quiet just for a moment so he could think clearer. "No one I know is. I can see you don't want to work with me to stop this so I'm going to leave now. But I promise you, I am going to find out what is happening in Maran, and if a Naga is behind it, I will stop him."

Kanvar twisted away from the palm tree, lifting his hunting knife to block Chandran's sword if Chandran should come at him, but Chandran did not strike.

Kanvar scooped up the iron box with Akshara's stone and limped away, his shoulders tense and ears straining to hear if Chandran made a move to attack him from behind.

"Kanvar," Chandran said.

Kanvar turned back, readying to fight for his life.

Chandran's face had softened just a bit. "I'm sorry we have to be enemies."

Kanvar's throat tightened. "I'm sorry too."

## Chapter Seven

**D**evaj woke to the sound of muted voices and a splitting headache. His father's mind cocooned his own in a thick shield that cut out stray thoughts from every creature and human other than Elkatran. When Devaj tried to lift his hand to his head, he found he'd been wrapped in warm blankets and tucked into his bed at home in the golden palace. Relieved, he nestled deeper into the soft mattress and wondered why Kanvar could fly off all over the world without getting hurt, but every time he left the palace he came back almost dead. At least he felt dead, the icy stab of Khalid's soul trying to force its way into him would not soon fade to the back of his mind.

*Kanvar does not come back unscathed either*, Elkatran corrected him. *He was badly burned on his trip to the Great North, and he and Dharanidhar nearly died in that hurricane on their way to Darvat. Whereas we made it to Darvat and back with Karishi without any trouble.*

Devaj cracked his eyes and looked over to the section of the chamber where Elkatran lay curled on the gold floor. Elkatran let out a playful puff of joy breath in his direction.

"Hey," Grandfather Raza's deep voice rumbled. "Parmver and I are trying to work here. The last thing we need is all that sparkly stuff turning our thoughts to mush."

Devaj twisted his gaze back to his own space and saw that Parmver and Kumar Raza had stretched several scrolls out across his desk and were in the process of looking them over.

"The water damage is unfortunate," Parmver said running his finger down the closest scroll.

"But they're still readable for the most part," Kumar Raza said. He leaned closer to inspect the scroll in front of him.

Parmver rubbed his gnarled hands together. "We've got to go back there."

"It won't do any good. The whole section of the palace collapsed down on that library."

"I can't believe it's still there. I thought it had been looted and destroyed like everything else in the palace. It will be well worth it to dig it back out. I'm going to talk to Haidar and Liander and see if they can engineer a way."

Devaj blinked. He figured he should ask Parmver for some tonic to relieve his headache, but he was still too groggy to make the effort.

Raza straightened. "I don't understand this map at all, Parmver. Why does it have two separate circles? The one on the left is clearly the map of the world, but this circle on the right is just gibberish."

Parmver chuckled. "Haven't you ever seen a globe? No...well, I suppose you haven't. The circle on the right is the back side of the world."

"What, the underside? You mean if we flip the world over there is something underneath us?"

"Not the underside. The back side. I suppose you picture the world as flat?"

"Of course it's flat." Raza raked his fingers through his beard and glared at Parmver.

Devaj stifled a laugh, remembering having a similar conversation with Parmver not long after coming to the palace to live.

Parmver rolled his eyes and tapped the scroll. "You picture it flat because the map is flat. Here, let me help you. Lay your hand palm down on the desk."

Scowling, Raza put his hand down.

Parmver uncapped Devaj's ink well and drew a map on the back of Raza's hand. "See this is the world you know: Varna, Maran, Kundiland, the Great North. Right?"

"Yes."

"Good. Now make you hand into a fist."

Raza lifted his hand and balled it into a fist.

Parmver tapped the back of his fist. "This is the part of the world you know. And this—" Parmver traced his finger around to the other side of Raza's fist, "—is the part of the world you've never seen. But I have. When I was young, some friends and I decided to make a complete circuit of the globe from Stonefountain eastward all the way back to Stonefountain. Because of dragon flight, Naga civilization was never limited to the world the humans know today." Parmver brought his finger the rest of the way around Raza's fist to the place he'd first pointed.

Kumar Raza stared at his fist for a long moment before saying anything. "Round," he finally muttered. "The world is round."

"Yes."

Devaj chuckled.

Both men whipped around to look at him.

"You're awake," Parmver said, his eyes twinkling.

"It's about time," Kumar Raza said.

"How did I get back here?"

"Elkatran and I brought you, of course."

"But Kanvar. I remember Kanvar was there. Was I dreaming?"

"No. He was there. He looked into your mind and explained to me what happened at the fountain with Khalid. Unfortunately I could not convince him to come back here with us."

"What?" Devaj jerked to a sit. "You let him go off to meet with the Maranies alone? We were supposed to follow him."

Kumar Raza frowned. "You were in no condition. It was all Elkatran and I could do to get you back here."

"But why didn't you stop Kanvar?"

"Elkatran and I are no match for Dharanidhar. There was nothing we could do."

"Kumar Raza is right," Parmver interrupted. "He had to bring you back here. How are you feeling?"

Devaj put his hand to his head. It hurt even worse since he sat up, and he wished he hadn't. "My head hurts. Do you have a tonic?"

"Yes, of course. I'll be right back." Parmver grabbed his cane from where it leaned against the desk and hobbled out of the room.

Raza glanced once more at the map inked on the back of his hand. "Round," he muttered and went back to looking at the scrolls.

"Anything useful there?" Devaj asked. He wanted to get up and look at the scrolls himself, but his body refused.

"Parmver was excited over this one." Raza eased one of the scrolls from the desk and turned it so Devaj could see the colorfully illuminated pictures and flourished script. But the edges were smeared in places."

"It got wet?"

"Yes, we went for a swim in the river, remember. It was the only way to get out of the chamber after everything crashed down outside."

"Right." Devaj had vague memories of that. He rubbed his head again and blinked. The room was starting to blur.

"Perhaps you should lie back down," Kumar Raza said, returning the scroll to the desk and coming over to ease Devaj back onto the bed.

"What did Parmver say was special about that scroll?" Devaj asked as Raza tucked the blankets back around him. "We have many illuminated manuscripts here already."

"It is an account of some ancient legendary Naga hero named Nikeron. Parmver says the original telling of the story dates back to the early days of Stonefountain. It seems the story of Nikeron is one of Parmver's favorites. Supposedly this hero lived five lifetimes."

"Five lifetimes, how?"

"Apparently his dragons kept dying, but there happened to be a new one there at the moment of death each time for Nikeron to bond with, and the new bond kept him alive."

"Impossible," Devaj said. But what about Kanvar, he thought. Maybe I can save him if Dharanidhar dies too soon.

"Yes, probably impossible. Parmver isn't sure that the story is even true. He thinks it may just be a work of ancient fiction, or in the very least an overly-embellished tale with only a tiny kernel of truth at its center."

"I'd like to read that scroll," Devaj said as Parmver hobbled back into the room with a steaming cup of a tonic for his headache.

"It's not quite dry yet," Raza said. "That's why we've got them rolled out here across your desk."

Devaj accepted the medicine and drank it slowly. It went down sweet and smooth, banishing his headache.

Dharanidhar landed clumsily in his and Kanvar's chambers at the gold palace. Shaking, he slid into his rocky nest and lay down. Kanvar unbuckled himself and climbed from his neck, but his legs gave out on him when his feet hit the ground. Dharanidhar was too tired to shield him from the constant pain in his legs, and Kanvar knew for sure that Dhar had lied about flying not hurting any more than sleeping. They had almost not made it back home from Darvat.

*I'm sorry*, Dharanidhar rumbled.

*Not your fault, Dhar.* Kanvar pulled himself back to his feet, keenly aware of the humiliation Dharanidhar felt at being so incapacitated. He especially feared what his old enemy, Rajahansa, would do if he found out how weak he'd become.

*Get some rest. I'm going to talk to Parmver about something to ease the pain.* Kanvar thought about cleaning up before he met with the other Nagas, but he could already feel them headed toward him. He needed to draw them away from Dharanidhar.

The pain of each step was nearly blinding as Kanvar limped down the golden hall. He kept his good hand on the wall to steady himself and blinked the sweat out of his eyes.

Grandfather Raza reached him first. "Kanvar, you're hurt. What's wrong?"

"I'm not hurt," Kanvar said. He turned in a circle. "See. Nothing wrong. Not a scratch."

"You met with Chandran?"

"Yes, I did."

Kanvar's father, dressed in flowing golden robes, came next. "Kanvar." He grabbed Kanvar in a tight hug. "Thank the Fountain you're alive."

Kanvar threw up the strongest shield his mind could create to block knowledge of the pain from his father and Rajahansa. Still, he could not stifle a gasp.

His father released him, but grabbed his shoulders and steadied him when he almost lost his balance. "What's wrong, son?"

Kanvar wiped the sweat out of his eyes and steadied his breathing. "Dhar's just tired from flying so far. We were trying to hurry back."

Parmver and his two sons joined them.

"General Chandran did not try to harm me," Kanvar blurted out before they could say anything. "It was not a trap. He just gave me some vital information and asked for our help." While not totally true, Kanvar figured his explanation would be the most likely to gain the support and help of the other Nagas.

"Help with what?" Haidar folded his arms across his chest.

Kanvar licked his lips. He did not know how the others would react or if they'd even believe him. "Chandran says a Naga has taken over the Maran government and is massing his entire army and navy at Wareham."

Red crept up Kumar Raza's neck and spread across his face. "The whole Maran army at Wareham. That's directly across the strait from Daro. It means—"

"War." Kanvar said. "I've thought about it all the way home. And I don't think Daro is his main target." Kanvar shuddered. "He's already taken over Maran. If he conquers Daro…well, where else would a Naga bent on ruling the world go but Stonefountain, the ancient seat of Naga power."

"No!" Parmver said.

Kanvar jumped back in surprise and nearly toppled over. He had never heard Parmver shout before. But Kanvar wanted to shout along with him. "Khalid is there, waiting to take over some Naga's body so he can live again. He almost had Devaj, but Devaj is young and not that powerful. I cannot even imagine the strength and power this rogue Naga must have to take over the Maran government. How could he have kept the Naga hunters from recognizing what he is and killing him? Surely they must know. Chandran was adamant that what was happening in the Maran Senate had to be the work of a Naga. Wouldn't everyone else feel the same? Why haven't the Maranies stopped him?"

"Hold on now." Kanvar's father motioned for everyone to stay calm. "Let's talk this out. Kanvar has brought up some good points. Chandran's allegations could be false. It does not seem possible that any Naga could use his powers so openly and not be killed."

"No, I think Chandran's right," Kanvar said. "I only brought up those questions because until we understand how he's done what he's done, we won't be able to think of a way to stop him."

"Kanvar, you're a fool." Haidar let out a little laugh. "And Chandran thinks the rest of us are as well. I see now what he's up to. Why catch the the Naga hatchling when you can use him for bait to slaughter the whole pride? He tells you there is a Naga in Maran, thinking we'll all come to meet him. And when we come to Wareham, every Naga hunter with every singing stone in Maran will be there waiting for us."

Kanvar shook his head. "You don't know Chandran like I do."

"You don't know anything," Haidar snarled. "You're just a child, barely over a decade and a half old. You know nothing of the world, and you'd do well to listen to the wisdom of us who have lived over eight centuries." Haidar motioned to himself and his brother. "Or our father who has lived over a thousand years."

"But—"

"Hold your tongue, Kanvar. Let the rest of us sort this out," Liander snapped.

Anger welled up in Kanvar and rushed out in a flood. "You think because I'm a cripple that I'm stupid too, but I'm not. I may be young, but I've been out in the world more than you. You, who have lived your whole life in the pampered safety of these gilded halls."

"We built these halls."

*Silence, both of you.* Rajahansa joined them, spreading his wings in warning.

Kanvar stumbled back against the wall and was glad for its support to relieve some of the pressure on his aching legs.

Haidar took a deep breath and dropped his gaze to his feet in submission.

*Haidar is right*, Rajahansa said. *This is no doubt a trap for all of you, thought up by the Maranies. But Kanvar, think just for a moment, even if* you *are right and there is another Naga out there, we* don't need to be the ones to stop him. The humans are very adept at hunting and killing Nagas. They've managed to slaughter our kind for a thousand years without our help. There is no way this Naga will make it to Stonefountain.*

Kanvar bit his lip. Fighting with Rajahansa would get him nowhere. He pushed away from the wall and limped back toward his own chambers.

*I forbid you to go after this Naga*, Rajahansa told him.

Kanvar whirled back around to face the Great Gold Dragon King. "You forbid me?"

*Yes.*

A ferocious roar shook the palace, and Dharanidhar lumbered out of his chamber. Coming to stand behind Kanvar, he raised himself up on his back legs, spread his wings and roared again in challenge.

Kanvar winced at the pain in their legs and drew his hunting knife from its sheath at his waist. "Dharanidhar is ready to fight to the death for our freedom," Kanvar said, pointing his knife at Rajahansa. "For death and glory, we will fight you all. And we will never stop fighting as long as there is any chance that King Khalid will once again rule this world."

Rajahansa sucked in a breath, readying to blow his joy breath at Kanvar and Dharanidhar.

Dharanidhar sucked in a breath as well. *Your joy breath might subdue me, but not before everyone one in this halls burns to ash.*

Kanvar shuddered. He would survive since he still wore his armor, and Kumar Raza had his armor on as well. Kanvar did not want to see his father and the other Nagas die though. He said as much into Dharanidhar's mind, but Dharanidhar just laughed at him.

*What's it going to be, Rajahansa?* Dharanidhar said. *I'm ready to die. Are you?*

*If you and Kanvar go after this Naga. You will die*, Rajahansa said, but he held his joy breath in.

*Kanvar and I are already dead.* Flames licked the edges of Dharanidhar's mouth.

"Rajahansa, Dharanidhar, please stop." Amar moved out between the two dragons. "There is no need for this arguing and certainly no need for fighting. Dharanidhar, you and Kanvar are free to come and go from this palace as you like. Rajahansa spoke a little too forcefully, but only out of concern for your welfare. He cares for you and does not want to see you murdered by the Maranies. It is clear that your freedom is more dear to you than life. Go if you like. We won't try to stop you." He swept a stern gaze over Haidar and Liander. Both men glared at Kanvar but said nothing.

Dharanidhar dropped to all fours, relieving some of the pressure on his hind legs. *Thank you.* He bowed to Amar then returned to his chamber. Kanvar kept his eyes locked on the hall in front of him so Dharanidhar could see his way back. Dhar barely got out of sight past the door before he slumped to the ground unconscious.

Kanvar's heart felt like ice. His hunting knife slipped from his cold fingers and clattered to the floor, cutting a gouge in the gold leafing. His father had given him permission to go after the rogue Naga, but it was clear none of the other Nagas would help him, and Dharanidhar would not fly again any time soon.

## Chapter Eight

**"H**ey, what's going on?" Devaj came down the hall rubbing groggy eyes. "Kanvar, you're back. Are you all right?"

Kanvar's throat felt too tight to answer. Leaving his knife where he'd dropped it and steadying himself against the wall, he limped back to his chambers. He thought about closing the huge wooden doors behind him, but figured he wouldn't be able to budge them. That would take Dharanidhar or one of the other dragons. He settled for squeezing under Dhar's limp wing to hide and hoping everyone would go away.

*Kanvar?* Devaj called to him.

*Leave me alone,* Kanvar answered then blocked his mind from Devaj and slumped against Dharanidhar's scaly side. At least while Dhar was unconscious Kanvar couldn't feel the pain. "Dhar," he whispered. "We have to stop this Naga. You know we have to stop this Naga. Tell me how."

"Kanvar?" It was Grandfather Raza's voice this time. He'd followed Kanvar into his chambers.

Kanvar remained silent and hidden beneath Dharanidhar's wing. He felt his grandfather circle the unconscious dragon then stride out of the room.

Devaj waited in the hall with Parmver while Kumar Raza went in to check on Kanvar. From the looks on everyone's faces when he'd arrived, Devaj figured something nasty had happened between Kanvar and the other Nagas. Rajahansa had been shaking with fury as he strode away. Haidar and Liander looked equally angry and started to say something to their king, but Amar cut them off and motioned for them to follow him to another part of the castle.

Parmver hobbled over to Devaj. "How are you feeling? How is your head?"

"Better," Devaj answered. "What happened here?"

"Kanvar believes that some Naga has taken over the Maran government and seeks to conquer the world and claim the throne at Stonefountain," Parmver said.

"Uh-oh. Khalid—"

"Yes, I know," Parmver said. "That's the problem. But Rajahansa forbade Kanvar to get involved, and Dharanidhar threatened to roast us all. I thought he might actually do it there for a moment."

Devaj clenched his fists. "That dragon is crazy, just crazy. I wish Kanvar had never bonded with him."

Kumar Raza strode out of Kanvar's chambers. His suntanned face had turned white. He raked his fingers through his beard and blinked as if trying to get a hold of himself before speaking.

"What is it?" Parmver said.

"I…" Kumar Raza looked over his shoulder back toward the chamber. "I don't think Dharanidhar was being melodramatic when he said he and Kanvar were already dead."

Devaj's chest tightened in fear, and he raced for the chamber. When he came through the arched doorway, he found Dharanidhar fallen just beyond. He lay unmoving and his ancient body seemed to struggle to draw in each breath. Devaj couldn't see or feel Kanvar anywhere.

"Parmver!" Devaj yelled, shaken. *Oh Parmver, hurry. Do something.*

Parmver hobbled into the room along with Grandfather Raza.

"What's wrong with him?" Raza said. "Do you think the Maranies poisoned him? I don't see any new wounds or scars."

"Parmver, you have to save them, somehow please. Where's Kanvar." Devaj's heart raced and he circled the chamber looking for Kanvar.

"Devaj, settle down," Parmver said. "Panicking doesn't help anything. Dharanidhar is clearly not dead, so there is no reason for hysterics."

Parmver's words did little to calm Devaj. "Kanvar," he called. "Kanvar, please, where are you? Come on, little brother, the other Nagas aren't here. It's just Parmver, me, and Grandfather."

Parmver walked to Dharanidhar and ran his hand down the old dragon's chest, which he could only reach because Dharanidhar lay sprawled on the floor. Then he checked his forelegs, wings, and hind legs in a similar manner. "His back legs are swollen as well as the joints in his wings." Parmver furrowed his eyebrows. "I'll need to make a draught to take down the inflammation. We'll need a lot of it. He's very large. I'll send some of the younger golds to gather the herbs."

"Do you think it will help?" Devaj asked.

Parmver huffed. "If it didn't, Ceiron and I would have died long ago. You have no idea what it's like to be old."

"No, sir. I guess not. I'm sorry. But does that mean Dhar and Kanvar will be all right?"

"Most likely yes." Parmver poked his head in between Dhar's wing and his body. "Did you hear that Kanvar. You're going to be fine. Both of you. It will just take time to treat, that's all. Give it a while and you'll both be flying again."

Kanvar struggled out from behind Dharanidhar's wing and slumped against his shoulder. "I don't have a while. I have to leave now, or I'll get to Maran too late to stop this Naga."

Devaj shook his head. "We are not Naga hunters. Chandran has the whole Maran army at his command, surely he is in a better position to handle this. Besides, you don't want to kill one of our own kind, do you?"

Kanvar lifted his good hand in protest. "Not kill him. I want to get to him before Chandran and convince him to stop interfering with the humans. He probably thinks he's the last, the only Naga in the world, just like Karishi did. Perhaps if he knows there are more of us, that there is a safe place to stay, he'll come back here with me and no one has to die. Don't you think we should at least find him and give him a chance?"

Parmver patted Kanvar's shoulder. "You've a kind heart, Kanvar. But it's been my experience that when a Naga turns bad, there's no turning him back. Believe me, I watched Khalid spiral into depravity. Nothing I said or did made any difference to him."

"But."

"I know. It's useless to argue with you," Parmver said, hobbling toward the door. "You don't want to listen to anyone. It's always that way with the young. You think you know more than any ancient relic who has already walked your path."

Kanvar tried to protest again, but Parmver waved it off. "I'm going to work on the medicine for Dharanidhar. I should have it done by the time he wakes."

"What if he doesn't wake?" Devaj said. "I'm going to lose my little brother."

"Nonsense." Parmver disappeared out into the hall.

"Devaj?" Kanvar turned hopeful eyes on him. "Will you ask Elkatran to carry me to Maran? He doesn't need to stay. Just get me there."

Devaj looked away. "Rajahansa has forbidden it. None of the gold dragons will disobey his command." Devaj felt bad, but Elkatran was one of Rajahansa's favorite sons. He would never go against his father's will.

Kumar Raza walked over to Kanvar and slid his fallen hunting knife into the sheath at his waist. "You're thinking about this wrong. We need to go to Varna. Going to Maran would be useless. The moment the Naga took over, he had to have moved to secure all the singing stones. Most of the Maranies keep theirs locked up in family storerooms and such. He sent the soldiers to seize them. If there anyone left in Maran with a singing stone, they would have already tried to use it, and failed I assume since you say the Naga is still in charge."

"Chandran has a singing stone. He's wearing it hidden beneath his armor." Kanvar ran his fingers along his knife hilt. That simple gesture made Devaj shudder.

"Good. We need an ally. Hopefully he's smart and will stay free of the Naga's grasp," Kumar Raza said.

"If there really is a Naga," Devaj said.

Kanvar opened his mouth to argue, but Kumar Raza spoke first. "If General Chandran says there is a Naga, then there is one. He has no reason to lie. Haidar's theory that it's some elaborate trap only makes sense in the mind of someone who knows nothing about hunting or trapping. If you have to defeat more than one dangerous dragon, you split them up and come on them alone. Take them out one at a time. Together they'd be too strong to defeat. But Chandran didn't attack Kanvar when he had him vulnerable and alone. The fact that he let Kanvar walk away, means that Chandran is telling the truth. There's a Naga. He's powerful, and the Maranies can't stop him."

"Chandran said he was going to try. Of course he wouldn't believe me that it wasn't one of us." Kanvar tried to stand on his own and walk away from Dharanidhar, but the effort seemed to cost him too much, and he fell back against the dragon.

Devaj jumped forward, put his arm under his brother's shoulders and led him over to his bed. He tried to get Kanvar to lie down, but Kanvar insisted on sitting.

"Why go to Varna?" Kanvar asked. "What good will that do?"

"The dragon hunters," Raza said. "He's got to hit the dragon hunter jati hard and fast. He knows they know he's a Naga. They have the singing stones and they know how to hunt him. That's why he's gathering the whole army around him. The problem is, the Varnans will think the pending attack will be aimed at their own military garrisons as it always has been in the past. I have to go and warn them that the strike will bypass the garrisons and hit the dragon hunter jati complex."

Devaj's head swam. The talk of wars and singing stones and fighting made him uncomfortable.

Grandfather Raza clapped him on the back. "You don't have to come, Devaj, and I'm not going to ask you or Elkatran to go against Rajahansa's wishes. But his Majesty never said you couldn't fly Kanvar and I down to the Varnan colony here in Kundiland. We can be packed in a few minutes, and Elkatran can have us there before nightfall. By morning we'll be on our way across the water in the fastest boat in port."

Devaj backed away. "I-I don't know."

"Rajahansa won't mind. You've flown me down to the Varnan colony a dozen times. He just doesn't want you to go to Maran because he fears for your life. There is no danger in a short flight down the coast."

Grandfather Raza checked over the weapons Kanvar carried. "Everything looks good. I'll be back in a minute."

"You're not going to take no for an answer are you?" Devaj said.

"That's right, I'm not. Have Elkatran meet us in the entry hall." Grandfather Raza strode out of the room.

Devaj shook himself. "I'm going to be in so much trouble."

Kanvar reached out and grabbed his hand. "Please, Devaj."

Devaj's heart melted. Kanvar had given up his entire life for him. "All right, Kanvar. I'm sorry you're hurting. I'm sorry Dharanidhar is…not well. I'm just afraid you're going to get yourself killed. It makes sense for Grandfather to go. He used to be head of the dragon hunter jati. But you're a Naga, and everyone is going to be after Nagas. And what help will you be?"

Kanvar gave Devaj a thin smile. "Grandfather is forgetting one thing. The Naga will send the army after the dragon hunters. The attack on Daro will trigger a meeting of the All Council. The council will gather in the council chambers, and the Naga will be there. While the dragon hunters are fighting the Maran army, no one will be able to stop the Naga from taking control of the All Council just like he did the Maran Senate. No one but me, that is. If I pose as a servant, I can get in there. The All Council always takes food and drink when they convene. No one will question a crippled untouchable as a servant. What other use would there be for me?"

Sweat broke out on Devaj's palms. His brother meant to go up against this powerful Naga alone. "Kanvar, you can't. You haven't learned enough from Parmver yet to fight this guy's mind. Dharanidhar might be strong enough but he's…he won't be there to help you."

"I know." Kanvar pulled an iron box from a leather pouch at his waist.

Devaj stumbled back. It was the largest singing stone box he had ever seen. "Don't open it. Where did you get that?"

"It's Akshara's. The one the blue dragons used on you when you were their prisoner."

Devaj shuddered. "Don't do this, Kanvar. Please don't do this."

Kanvar returned the box to the pouch and stood. "Do you know where Tana is?"

"Yes."

"I need to talk to her before I leave."

"Her chambers are in the west wing near the back. Are you strong enough to walk there? Do you want my help?"

Grimacing, Kanvar stood on his own. "I can't feel the pain when he's unconscious. My head's not swimming anymore. I'll be fine. Thank you, Devaj." Kanvar gave him a one-armed hug then limped out the door.

Devaj watched him leave then turned to stare at the crumpled blue dragon. He shook his head. "I'm going to go read that scroll one more time. There has to be a way to undo this madness."

Kanvar limped through the palace to the west wing. He saw no one and suspected that all the Nagas and dragons were avoiding him. The fact that Dharanidhar had threatened to kill every Naga in the palace beside Devaj and Karishi had probably made them all so mad they'd never speak to Kanvar again. It made him sad and nervous. Now that he and Dharanidhar were exiled from the blue dragon pride, they had no other home than here. No other safe place to go, and Dharanidhar needed somewhere safe to recover, someone like Parmver to heal him.

The smell of gold permeated everything and made Kanvar nauseous. He hoped no one would try to harm Dharanidhar while he was away.

Hearing soft female voices behind a door up ahead, he stopped and knocked. After a moment, his mother answered it.

"Kanvar, you're back safe I see." She gave him a hug. "I told your father not to worry so much. You've proved you can take care of yourself."

His mother looked far better than she had when she'd first come to the palace. Her silky hair reflected the gold light, and her cheeks had a healthy sheen to them. It made Kanvar glad to see her healthy and happy, but inside he recoiled from her touch. She had tried to kill him, and though he wanted to forgive her for that, he had not yet been able to. He stepped away from her grasp and asked after Tana.

"She's inside, of course. Come in. She, Eska, and I were just planning a party to celebrate Tana coming here." She motioned for the door, but Kanvar made no move to enter.

"I-I'd like to talk to her alone."

A twinkle and a smile came to his mother's face. "You do, do you? Well...of course. I'll send her right out."

She disappeared into the room. Sweat slicked the inside of Kanvar's gauntlets, and he licked his lips.

Tana stepped out of the room, wearing a flowing blue dress. It accented her gray skin and made her long black hair shimmer. The effect was striking and warmed him.

"Tana, I'm sorry," he blurted out before she could say anything. "I didn't mean to tell anyone your secret. It just came out all wrong. I only wanted to help you, to keep you safe."

Tana reached out and took his crippled hand in hers. He flinched, but she held it too tight for him to pull away.

"Dearest Kanvar. You are so sweet. I know I was angry, but I understand now. This place is beautiful. You must love living here."

Kanvar grimaced. "I'm going to love seeing you here."

Tana frowned. "You seem unhappy."

"I've argued with Rajahansa again. All the other Nagas are angry with me. I'm sorry Tana, but I don't think I will ever be welcome here." Kanvar lifted his good hand to brush her cheek. "But you'll be all right here. Just do what they say and...act like the rest of them." Kanvar looked away and dropped his hand. Just because he had become an outcast didn't mean she had to be unhappy living an easy life at the palace.

Tana squeezed his hand. "Kanvar, what are you saying? Everyone loves you here. Your mother, your father, Eska and Denali, Devaj, Parmver. They all speak highly of you. You're a hero to them."

Kanvar choked. If she only knew the truth. "Well, I'm afraid I have to go off and be heroic one more time. I'll be leaving for Varna with Kumar Raza in a few minutes. I just wanted to make sure you're all right and say goodbye before I leave."

"Kanvar, don't go away again." Tana pressed against his chest and looked into his face.

"I'm sorry. I have to." Warmth spread across his chest, up his neck, and over his face. He wrapped his good arm around her, kissed her forehead, then pulled away. "Goodbye, Tana."

She tried to hold onto him, but he pulled free and limped away. After a moment he heard the door slam behind him. No one would ever understand him. He shook his head and limped toward the front entry hall.

As he came around a curve, he ran into Bensharie, pacing out in the hall. Bensharie startled back, his wings flaring. *Kanvar, you're here? How was your trip? The Maran general didn't hurt you did he?*

"Of course not. Chandran was like a father to me." Kanvar tried to limp around Bensharie, but the young gold dragon put a forepaw on his chest.

*Kanvar, I've been wanting to talk to you. My chamber is right here. Will you come in for a minute?*

"I'm in a hurry, Bensharie." Kanvar tried to keep the impatience out of his voice.

*Please.*

"Bensharie, I'm sorry I yelled at you. I know you saved my life. Thank you. I'm grateful. I need to go now."

Bensharie lowered his head. His wings and shoulders slumped in disappointment. He shuffled into the closest chamber and closed the door down to a crack that only a human could get through.

Kanvar took a deep breath. He did owe Bensharie his life. Grandfather Raza would probably not be too angry if Kanvar spoke with Bensharie for a moment. Kanvar slipped into the dragon's chambers and looked around. The room stunned him. He expected the gold-covered walls and floor. They were the same everywhere in the palace, except in his own chamber. But in the center of the room where Bensharie nested, a down-filled mattress was laid and spread with several fluffy comforters. A crystal chandelier hung from the ceiling, refracting the sunlight from the window in an array of rainbow streaks along the walls. A wooden bookcase, carved with jungle scenes, stood up against one wall. Beside it, sat a matching desk with stacks of paper, several empty inkwells, even more full ones, and a dozen quill pens.

With his back to Kanvar, Bensharie growled, snatched up one of the quill pens and stabbed it into the closest inkwell.

"Bensharie?" Kanvar hoped he hadn't made Bensharie too angry with him, since Bensharie seemed to be the only gold dragon still willing to talk to him.

Bensharie whirled around, the pen forgotten in his hand, dripping ink on the desk, the dragon, and the floor. *Kanvar?*

"I'm sorry I was rude. What did you want to tell me?" Kanvar leaned against the wall to steady his tired legs.

Bensharie bowed to Kanvar. *Thank you for your time, Your Highness. I have written a poem inspired by your battle with the volcanic dragon and thought you might like to hear it. It's titled "The Farmer and the Dragon."*

Kanvar chuckled. "I'm not a farmer."

*No. Of course you aren't.* Bensharie fluttered his wings. *It's not about you, it was just inspired by you. Have you studied poetry and literature?*

"I've never read a poem in my life."

Bensharie cocked his head. *But you can read?*

"Of course I can."

*Good. Good. May I read this poem to you?* Bensharie lifted a paper from the desk and held it in front of his face.

"I'd love to hear it." Kanvar tapped his fingers against his knife hilt and hoped the poem wouldn't be too long. Grandfather Raza would be waiting for him in the entry hall.

Bensharie's dragonstone brightened to a brilliant gold as he recited the poem to Kanvar.

*Swift dragon death*
*by fire and flame.*
*You went to meet the monster.*
*With sacred sword*
*you stood alone,*
*icicle fire along your bones,*
*sweat seared dry,*
*encompassed by inferno.*
*Oh, cowardly courage.*
*Dear death to die in glory.*
*You feared only*
*the unheralded dull dread toil*
*of plow and stone and soil.*

Bensharie's words slid like liquid fire through Kanvar's mind, and tears sprang to his eyes. A heavy weight on his chest made it hard for him to breathe. In a few simple lines Bensharie had captured Dharanidhar's greatest anguish—to live on, doing nothing of value when he should have died a glorious death as the leader of the blue dragon pride.

Kanvar gasped for the air that refused to fill his lungs.

Bensharie dropped the paper and crossed the chamber to Kanvar. *Are you hurt?*

Kanvar pressed his hand to his chest and shook his head, but he couldn't speak for a moment. Back in Daro, the dragon hunters had always made fun of the scholars and their poetry. He wished now he might have taken some time to understand it. "How? How did you know that? Dhar and I haven't told anyone?"

Bensharie sat back on his haunches. *Told anyone what?*

Kanvar shuddered. He hadn't thought there would be anyone in the palace he dared tell about Dharanidhar's exile, but he felt suddenly that Bensharie might understand. "Dharanidhar is supposed to be dead. The blue dragon pride decided he was too old and crippled to continue to lead them. He was supposed to fight to the death to make way for a younger, stronger leader. Instead he accepted the greatest humiliation a Great Blue dragon can face, voluntary exile. For me, because he thinks I'm too young to die. He goes on living, old and hurt and useless…unheralded dull, dread, toil. Bensharie, why did you write that poem?"

Bensharie stepped back and looked Kanvar up and down before speaking. *I-I don't think you'll understand.* He picked up the fallen paper and returned it and the still-dripping pen to the desk.

"What do you mean I won't understand? You can't insist on reading me a poem like that and then refuse to tell me why?"

Kanvar rubbed his head as Elkatran's voice came into his mind. *Where are you? We're ready to go.* Kanvar assured him he was coming, but stayed rooted in place waiting for Bensharie to explain himself.

Growling under his breath, Bensharie settled onto his haunches and pointed to a shelf filled with books. *See there, I have read dozens of books about heroes and their adventures.* He pointed to the next shelf down where four volumes with new-looking covers sat. *I have even made up my own heroes and written books and poetry about them. But it is all fiction, all lies. Look at me, I live in this*—he gestured to the room around him—*safe, luxurious palace. I go nowhere and do nothing heroic. What kind of hypocrisy is that, to write of heroism and live like a coward. But for one moment with you I got to live the way I dream. I got to face a volcanic dragon. I was so terrified I almost couldn't breathe my joy breath, but I did. When I'm with you, I am more than a scholar. Kanvar, I don't know where you're going, but please let me come with you?*

Kanvar cleared his throat. "Well, now I see why your father picked you as one of the possible dragons to bond with me. I couldn't figure it out before. I'm glad you and I got to fight that lesser volcanic dragon together. It was fun. But you can't come with me now. There is a Naga in Maran, evil and powerful. He's taken control of the humans, and I have to stop him. But your father has forbidden all of the Nagas and dragons from helping me. He thinks it is a Maranie trap, and anyone who goes will die. Kumar Raza and I have to deal with this on our own. I'm sorry, Bensharie, but you cannot come. Maybe when I return, if I survive, you and I can go on some other adventure together."

*My father forbade anyone to help you?* Bensharie's eyes widened in outrage. *He wants you to go alone?*

"He forbade me to go as well, of course. But I don't take orders from him." Kanvar gave Bensharie a grim smile. "I have to go. Kumar Raza is waiting for me. When I get back I'd like to hear some more of your poetry." Kanvar slipped out the crack in the door before Bensharie could argue with him further.

Kanvar would like to have had Bensharie fly him directly to Daro. It would be faster than the route Kumar Raza had planned, but Bensharie was too small to carry both Kanvar and his grandfather, and if Kanvar took Bensharie, Rajahansa would try to stop them.

When Kanvar stepped into the entry hall, Kumar Raza, Elkatran, and Devaj were waiting for him. Kumar Raza was already on Elkatran's back with a bundle of supplies behind him. Devaj stood in the center of the hall with Amar's sheathed sword in his hands.

Kanvar limped over to him. "Are you coming?"

Devaj shook his head. "Elkatran can fly faster with only two. Three people is hard for him, he's not that big. We're both young still."

"The sword?"

"For you." Devaj held it out to him. "Father wants you to take it."

"But what if I get killed? It would fall into enemy hands, and he won't have it for Denali's, Tana's, and Aadi's Bonding Ceremonies." Kanvar lifted the sword from his brother's hands. Even sheathed, power resonated in his grasp.

"Exactly. Father wants it to remind you that you have to come back alive. We need the sword, but more importantly we need you." Devaj clapped him on the back and walked with him over to Elkatran, who bent to the ground so Kanvar could get up in front of Kumar Raza.

Elkatran lifted his head, securing Kanvar in place and launched himself from the arched window. Kanvar twisted back as they flew away from the palace straining to see Dharanidhar through their chamber window. Dharanidhar's still lay unconscious in a heap on the floor. It didn't seem right to be flying without him, and the thought of facing a powerful Naga without the strength of Dharanidhar's mind to back him up made Kanvar shudder.

# Chapter Nine

**Kanvar leaned against the** ship's rail and watched the sun rise over Daro. Heat ripples undulated above the water and flowed across the docks. A ragged Varnan desert robe protected his skin from the brightness and covered his armor and sword. He'd left his crossbow with their other gear below.

A cloud of dust hung over the long rows of mud-brick buildings. His heart swelled at the sight of his childhood home. He loved Daro and was glad to be returning even under such dire circumstances.

"I'd forgotten about the constant dust," Kanvar said to his grandfather who stood beside him on the sleek merchant ship. It had made good time across the ocean. The captain had set all other concerns aside when Kumar Raza had explained to him about the threat set to launch against Daro. Still, Kanvar had feared they might come too late. But when they had entered the mouth of the channel all seemed to be well.

The captain strode up to Kumar Raza, carrying a spy glass.

Kanvar dropped his gaze to his feet and slumped submissively. He'd been posing as Kumar Raza's servant and was surprised how easily he'd fallen back into the role he'd played for so many years with Chandran.

"Have a look," the captain said, handing the glass to Kumar Raza and pointing across the channel toward Maran.

Kumar Raza focused the spy glass and swore. "They've launched the fleet. We're almost too late. How long until we dock?"

The captain grimaced. "I'd rather not be here when the fighting starts. This is a merchant ship, not a man-of-war. I'll have my men row you ashore now. Then we'll head back out of the channel."

"Excellent," Kumar Raza said. He turned a dismissive glare at Kanvar. "Stay here, boy. I'll go get my things. You are too slow and useless. Stupid. Don't know why I even bought your indenture."

Kanvar kept his eyes down and said nothing. Kumar Raza treated him harshly, but they'd both agreed it was necessary. No one in Daro was likely to have forgotten that Kumar Raza's crippled grandson was a Naga. Though Kanvar was supposed to be dead, he kept his face and deformities hidden by the robe and accepted Raza's pretend contempt, hoping no one would see through the disguise.

The sailors lowered a dingy to the water beside the ship. A moment later Kumar Raza returned to the deck carrying a bundle of their things. He shoved it at Kanvar who grabbed it one handed and slid it over his back.

The sailors flung a knotted rope over the side for Kumar Raza and his servant to climb down into the dingy. Kanvar's heart sunk. There was no way he could get down that rope while carrying their supplies on his back. Even without them he couldn't climb down without revealing his deformities.

Kumar Raza snorted. "The boy's too clumsy to climb down that. I'll just tie a rope around his middle and lower him like the lump of useless cargo he is." In a moment Raza had a rope around his middle. He lifted Kanvar over the side of the boat and dropped him.

Kanvar bit his lip to keep from crying out in fear, but he only fell a few feet before the rope around him snapped tight, and his grandfather and the sailors lowered him into the dingy. Then Kumar Raza came down followed by the sailors who took their place in the dingy and rowed to shore. When they reached the dock, Raza hefted Kanvar out of the boat, thanked the sailors, and waved them off.

"You all right?" Grandfather Raza asked him under his breath as he strode into the city, keeping his pace slow so that Kanvar's limp wouldn't be too noticeable.

"I'm fine." Kanvar's heart raced. As fine as he could be walking into a city where everyone would kill him instantly if they knew what he was.

"You remember the way to the All Council meeting hall?" Grandfather Raza asked.

Kanvar glanced up at the oval building on the hill at the center of the city and shrugged.

"Right. Stupid question. Can you walk that far. Dhar's legs still hurting?"

"I can't feel him. He's still unconscious. I'm worried about him." Each step Kanvar took brought him deeper into the narrow streets and throngs of people pouring into them.

"Worry about yourself."

Kanvar nodded, but kept his head submissively lowered in case anyone was watching.

Kumar Raza stopped at an intersection. "We split up here. You know what you have to do. Just subdue him and wait for me to join you. I'll come up to the meeting hall just as soon as I alert the military to the Maranies true target and get the dragon hunters safely out of the jati complex."

"Then what?" Kanvar didn't relish putting Akshara's singing stone on any Naga, but it seemed the only way to stop him.

"That depends on this Naga. If he's willing to sneak away quietly with us, we'll come back to the dock, steal a small boat, and sail back to Kundiland. If not, I'll have to turn him over to the dragon hunters. I hate to do it, but we can't let him go free."

"I don't like it," Kanvar said, "but I know you're right. Be well. Be careful."

"You too."

Kanvar started up the long road to the meeting hall. He kept his face hidden and his back hunched under the load he carried as he limped along. He was a cripple, yes, but hundreds of cripples worked as servants or begged in Daro's streets. Just one of so many. He willed people not to see him. Crippled. Untouchable. Below notice.

The dry heat made his lips crack as he wound his way up, and dust clung to his tongue. He grew thirsty, but though there was water with the supplies on his back, he let it be.

As he reached the steps of the meeting hall, the warning bell started tolling, announcing the Maranies attack. Kanvar glanced toward the dock and saw the water full of warships, the blue and gold Maran flags flapping like a flock of sea birds. The clash of weapons and cries of fighting wafted up to him.

He circled to the back of the building and joined the rush of servants climbing the narrow steps up to the servants' entrance. Heat waves rippled up the sculpted columns to the domed roof. If Kanvar were wrong, the Naga would never come here. He could be safely back with the senate in Wareham. He could be on the war ships. Or he could be leading the sneak attack on the dragon hunter jati.

No one stopped Kanvar as he entered the building. A rush of other servants came in with him. The ringing bell would bring the All Council to the meeting hall, and these illustrious men and women would expect to be served. Kanvar shuffled into the kitchen, left his bundle by the door, and joined the others in preparing food and drink for the All Council.

Working one handed, he readied a serving tray with sweet rice balls, cheeses, and flame broiled itchekin kabobs, preferring to stay away from carrying any of the drinks that his limping gate might spill. No one said anything to him or questioned his presence. He kept his hood over his face and his head down, like everyone else—the untouchable class trained into silent submission through a lifetime of ill treatment. When he had the tray ready, he fished the iron box from its pouch, set it next to the food, and covered it with a cleaning rag, a slightly dirty one so none of the All Council would grab it to wipe their fingers.

Easing the serving tray onto his shoulder and steadying it with his good hand, Kanvar limped out of the kitchen, through the hall, into the columned main chamber. A din of voices filled the room. Though Kanvar kept his head down he could tell from everyone's feet that no one had taken their places along the benches yet. There was fearful talk of unannounced war, speculation on why, and arguments over what should be done. Four representatives from every jati filled the chamber. Farmers and craftsman and scholars and merchants, doctors and fishermen and bards and more.

Kanvar shuffled among them, offering them food, keeping his face hidden, searching for a Naga's thoughts to surface above the mental chatter of the All Council members. He felt nothing, and as the minutes passed, his nervous stretched taut. He returned to the kitchen and refilled his tray then continued serving.

A door slammed open and a soldier's shrill voice shouted, "The ships are a decoy. The full Maran army just broke through the East Gate and descended on the dragon hunter jati complex. Kumar Raza is here. He says there's a Naga controlling them. It's trying to capture all the singing stones before they can be used against it."

The chamber erupted in yells of anger and fright. Then a soft voice cut through the room, slicing into everyone's mind. *Do not move.*

Kanvar found himself frozen in place. Though he'd been ready with his own shields, the Naga had taken him by surprise and he hadn't raised them fast enough.

The room fell silent except for the Naga who continued to speak. *There is no Naga.* The voice was young and male, rich with assurance. *You have nothing to fear. Make me your leader, and I will save you from the Maran invasion.*

Each word twisted Kanvar's mind with a subtle power, if the Naga's thoughts had been aimed at him, he knew he would be unable to resist the command, *do not fear, make me your leader.*

"Be our leader," someone cried out. "Save us."

Other voices joined the first.

*"Of course I will save you. Take your places. We will talk together and plan."*

At the Naga's command to take their places, Kanvar found he could move again. His place was to serve, and he was free to do it as the All Council shuffled into their seats.

Kanvar was overwhelmed by the skill with which the Naga controlled so many minds. He had to have been practicing the ability and building his power for a long time to achieve such mastery.

With the All Council in their seats, the Naga began to weave a new vision of the world for them. The power and glory of Stonefountain would rise again, with the Naga as the world's benevolent leader. The inventions and majestic artwork of the past would be restored. For the Unani doctors, he spoke of medicines that worked beyond their current understanding. For the scholars, he spoke of vast libraries of knowledge restored to their hands. For the bards, he spoke of lost ballads found and performed to throngs of happy listeners.

While the Naga spoke, Kanvar made his way along the benches toward the front of the room where the Naga stood. Kanvar had a job to do, to stop the Naga, but the Naga's spellbinding vision shimmered through his mind. It was his own vision. What he wanted more than anything, peace between humans and Nagas, civilization restored, the abuses of the past outlawed. No more slaves, just freedom and prosperity for all. This was a dream he could believe in. This was a cause he could fight for. And this Naga, unlike the cowards at the golden palace, was willing to do whatever it took to make it happen.

Still carrying the tray, Kanvar limped forward and knelt at the Naga's feet.

He felt the Naga look down at the tray of food. The roasted itchekin made the Naga hungry. He reached for one of the kabobs, but a deeper hunger stirred, hot and terrifying. He looked at Kanvar, and it was not the kabob he hungered for, but human flesh. The Naga's hungry passion opened his mind. He was a red dragon, basking in the burning magma at the volcanoes core. He was ravenous with a desire for human flesh that could not be satiated. He enjoyed pain and killing, fire and destruction, he would rule over humanity and have an endless supply of fresh blood.

The twisted horror of the Naga's mind churned Kanvar's stomach. He had never imagined the atrocities this Naga and his dragon had perpetrated, and the realization of what he intended for the world burned like liquid fire through Kanvar's veins.

He set the tray on the ground at the Nagas feet, threw off his robes, grabbed Akshara's singing stone by the chain from its box with his crippled left hand and drew his father's sword with his right.

The Naga let out a yell of rage, but Kanvar leaped on him, slamming him against the wall, dragging the singing stone's chain down over his head, and pressing the sword against his throat.

"Don't move," Kanvar said. "This sword cuts through dragon scales like cream. It is Khalid's sword and can sever your head with the flick of my wrist."

The Naga roared, sounding more dragon than human. He clawed at the singing stone hanging on his neck. The excruciating pain from the singing stone affected Kanvar as well, but he fought through the pain to keep control.

"Put you hands down." Kanvar pressed the blade so it cut into the Naga's neck. Blood seeped up around the edges of the blade. Kanvar looked the Naga in the eyes preparing to offer him the chance to leave the humans and come to Kundiland, but the face Kanvar stared into was familiar to him, indelibly imprinted in his mind from Kumar Raza's memories. Flaming blond hair, cheeks, nose, and mouth almost identical to Raza. But he was young, barely older than he had been in Raza's mind.

"Rajan?" Kanvar said. It was, it had to be, Kumar Raza's twin brother, but Rajan was supposed to be dead, murdered by his own uncle and father.

The Naga blinked at him as if the name meant nothing to him.

"Rajan. You are Rajan?" Kanvar's heart coiled tight with joy and despair. Kumar Raza's brother was alive, but when Kanvar had seen into Rajan's mind there had been no trace of the brother Kumar Raza remembered, there had only been red dragon bloodlust and cruelty. Kanvar's hand shook as it clutched the sword. "Come away with me," he said. "There are other Nagas. You don't need to conquer the humans. Let's leave this place together." The true Rajan had to be buried somewhere beneath the red dragon's mind.

Rajan bared his teeth and roared. He knocked the sword from Kanvar's hand and drew his own sword, swinging at Kanvar.

Kanvar dodged the blow and pulled out his hunting knife.

Shouts erupted in the chamber behind Kanvar as the singing stone broke the control Rajan had over the All Council members.

"He's a Naga!"

"Get him."

"Kill him."

Rajan tore the singing stone from around his neck, and Kanvar froze.

A firm hand grabbed Kanvar from behind and pulled him away from Rajan.

"It's all right. I've got him now," Chandran said.

Kanvar looked around and realized that a force of Maran soldiers had burst into the meeting hall.

Rajan shrieked, dropped the singing stone, and attacked Chandran.

Chandran met his attack with his own sword. The two fought, blade to blade, but Rajan was a cunning swordsman, skilled beyond anything Kanvar had seen before, and Chandran was no longer young. Rajan drove Chandran to his knees, and stabbed for Chandran's heart.

Kanvar dove between them, blocking the blow with his knife. A pair of Maran soldiers grabbed Rajan, bound his hands behind his back, put Akshara's singing stone over his head, and stuffed a gag into his mouth.

"No wait," Kanvar said.

"Why?" one of the soldiers asked. "What do you care?"

"He's a Naga too." One of the members of the All Council pointed a shaking finger at Kanvar. "I heard him talking to that one. They're working together."

Chandran grabbed Kanvar, slammed him up against the wall, and looped his own singing stone over Kanvar's neck. The pale high note of the tormented female spirit transfixed him. The soldiers tore the hunting knife from Kanvar's hand.

Chandran leaned in close to Kanvar's face and spoke in a low voice. "By law I must arrest you too and take you for execution before the senate along with this other Naga."

Kanvar shook his head in amazement. "I just saved your life. I stopped the Naga like I told you I would."

Chandran glanced at Rajan and grimaced then turned his attention back to Kanvar. "I'm sorry Kanvar." Chandran whispered. "You should have kept your mouth shut so no one else knew what you are. The best I can do is give you a chance to fight your way free." He pulled Kanvar away from the wall and flung him to the ground.

Kanvar's fingers closed on his father's sword, which had fallen in the spot where Chandran thrust him down.

Chandran swung at Kanvar, and Kanvar blocked it with his father's sword. When the two blades met, the Naga King's sword, imbued with the powers of Stone-fountain, severed Chandran's in half.

Chandran froze in shock for a split second, and Kanvar limped away, but the soldiers ringed him. Kanvar changed his course, heading for the closest pillar.

The soldiers closed in.

Kanvar sliced the sword diagonally through the stone pillar. The two pieces groaned and slid apart. The roof sagged, and several bricks toppled down.

While the soldiers cried out and dodged the bricks, Kanvar ran for the kitchen door. He grabbed his bundle of supplies as he limped out the servants' entrance. The stairs, ever his bane, slowed him.

The Maran soldiers and members of the All Council poured out of the building above him. Crossbows loaded, the soldiers aimed at him, and Kanvar knew his blue dragonscale armor would not deflect the bolts. He had no cover, and his own crossbow was bound up in the bundle on his back.

Grandfather Raza raced out of the street below and headed up toward him. A dozen dragon hunters followed on his heels

"He's a Naga," the Maran soldiers shouted, pointing at Kanvar. "Kill him."

Soldiers and dragon hunters took aim. Kanvar sucked in a breath. With the singing stone hanging around his neck, he could not feel Dharanidhar, awake or unconscious. His friend would not know that they had both died in glory, but Kanvar knew this was how Dharanidhar would prefer to end it. He squared his shoulders and lifted his head to look Chandran in the eyes as he fell.

"No," Kumar Raza shouted. "Let's take him alive, then we can burn him in front of the people. They'll want someone to blame for this attack. We can give it to them."

"You are not in charge," the head of the All Council called down to Raza. "I am, and I command you to kill him now. Kill them both this instant."

"Kill that one if you like," Chandran said. "But this one is going with me for trial and execution before the Maran Senate. I regret the attack on your city, but it was necessary to capture this Naga. I and my men will withdraw now without further conflict."

Kanvar looked down at his grandfather. He could see Raza's mind racing to think of some way to save him, but what could he do?

"Kill him. Fire those weapons," the head of the All Council shouted.

Kanvar steeled himself against the coming onslaught of crossbow bolts.

Hot air rippled from the roof of the meeting hall, a shower of golden sparkles blew into the faces of the soldiers, and sharp claws grabbed Kanvar by the shoulders, digging into his flesh as they jerked him off the ground straight up into the air. Up and up where the crossbow bolts from the dragon hunters couldn't reach him.

Then he flew, wind in his face, pain in his shoulders from the claws digging his flesh grappling to hold him, out of the city northeastward toward the channel. Blood from the claws trickled down his chest and back, and the singing stone filled his mind with sharp sorrow.

## Chapter Ten

**R**elief flooded through **Kumar Raza** as he watched the ripple of gold soar into the sky, carrying Kanvar. He did not know what Great Gold dragon had come to their aid, but by the fountain, he was glad. Still, Raza could not reveal himself as a Naga lover.

He shouted to the other dragon hunters. "Shoot the air above the Naga. You'll hit his dragon and bring them both down."

The other dragon hunters complied, but Raza had waited just long enough to shout that Kanvar and the gold dragon were out of their range.

Raza aimed his own crossbow, a more powerful weapon than any of theirs, and released two bolts. The first one clipped the dragon's right wing, and the dragon became visible for a moment.

Kumar Raza's heart sunk. The dragon was too small, one of the children, and it was already struggling to keep hold of Kanvar. The second bolt, already in the air, hit the center of its left wing. If the dragon had been the size Raza had imagined, the shot would have punched through the lower section of the wing without doing enough damage to stop the dragon. Instead it tore a large gash in the tender golden flesh.

The little dragon let out a pained yelp and spiraled down toward the water front.

"Good shot." The head of the dragon hunter jati clapped him on the back. "Let's go get him boys."

Kumar Raza shook his head. "The Maran army is there. They'll finish him long before we arrive." But that didn't stop him and the other dragon hunters from racing toward the docks.

Kanvar gritted his teeth as he tumbled with the dragon from the sky toward the ocean cliffs east of Daro. Waves pounded the jagged rocks below, sending up jets of white water. The claws in Kanvar's shoulders tore his flesh as the dragon flared its wings to slow the fall. But the hole in the dragon's wing disrupted the air flow and spun him and Kanvar around into the cliff. A jagged rift in the rock swallowed them.

The dragon snapped his wings tight against his sides barely in time to avoid them tearing off as they plunged into the dark crevice. Kanvar slipped from its claws and collided with wet stone. He thrust his father's sword away from himself so he wouldn't be cut as he rolled to a stop, scratched, bruised, and bleeding.

Cold ocean spray crashed into the narrow crack where they landed. Starfish and barnacles covered the rocks giving Kanvar the ominous understanding that this chamber filled with water when the tide came in.

He staggered to his feet and loosed the bundle of supplies he had strapped to his back. The song from the singing stone around his neck battered his mind as ferociously as the waves clashed against the rocks. He tore the chain off over his head and threw the stone far out into the heaving waves. The voice softened and then went silent as the undertow carried it out into the channel.

A pain-filled keening rose from the dragon behind him.

Kanvar turned and saw Bensharie crumpled against the rock at the back of the crevice. Blood trickled from his torn wing. The light from his dragonstone was so dim it hardly lit the chamber. He looked at Kanvar with pain-filled eyes and moaned.

"Bensharie." Kanvar limped over to the wounded dragon. "Rajahansa's going to kill me. What are you doing here? Does he know where you are?" Since Bensharie made no move to lick his wound closed, Kanvar pulled out his own vial of dragon saliva, gently pulled the torn flaps of skin together, and spread the viscous liquid across the rent.

*I followed you here.* Panting, Bensharie watched him work in too much shock from the pain to say more.

Kanvar used the last of the vial to heal over the nick on Bensharie's other wing, then he slumped to the ground next to his dragon friend. "Do you suppose they'll find us here? The tide's pretty high. Maybe they won't be able to get to us. If we're lucky, they'll think we crashed against the rocks and died."

Bensharie whimpered.

Grimacing, Kanvar removed his armor and examined the torn flesh where Bensharie's claws had dug into his shoulders. Blood trickled down his arms, chest, and back.

"Bensharie." Kanvar rubbed his hand across Benshar-ie's dragonstone, trying to calm him and get his attention. *Bensharie, we're safe now. It's all right.*

Gradually Bensharie's gaze became less clouded and he focused on Kanvar. *You're bleeding. Did I do that to you?*

"You saved my life, Bensharie. Thank you. That was incredibly heroic."

*But you're bleeding.* Bensharie shuddered.

Kanvar chuckled. "Yes. I noticed that. It would be a big help to me if you would lick these wounds closed. You're saliva can heal them. You do know that, right?"

Bensharie swallowed and licked his lips. *Yes, I'm sorry. I've read about that. How does it work?*

"Just lick my shoulders."

*But there's blood all over them. All over you. I-I feel faint. I can't lick blood. I'll vomit.* Shivering, Bensharie tucked his head under his wing.

"Heroic adventure's a little more than you bargained for is it?" Kanvar retrieved a soft cloth from his supply bundle and coaxed Bensharie's head back out from under his wing. "Never mind about licking. Let me just rub this cloth around the edges of your mouth for a moment."

Kanvar wet the cloth with dragon saliva and swathed it across his shoulders. The bleeding stopped and the sharp pain subsided to a dull ache. He took off his torn undershirt and washed himself, the undershirt, and his punctured armor in the frothing water that bubbled and hissed outside the chamber. Then he wiped his armor dry and put it on over a clean shirt from the bundle.

"Good thing Grandfather Raza knows what to pack." Kanvar inspected the rents in the shoulders of his armor where Bensharie's claws had gone through. "Well, you'd think the blue dragon scales would do a better job of warding off Great Gold dragon claws. I'm going to have to mend these holes." But he couldn't bring himself to pull out the leatherworking kit and get to work.

Panting, Bensharie stared at him with wide eyes.

"Still in shock." Kanvar limped back over to the dragon and rubbed his shoulder. "Are you hurt anywhere else? Any broken bones or cuts I can't see?"

*I-I'm all right now. Thank you.* Bensharie lowered his head to rest on his foreclaws. *I guess I'm not much of a hero.*

Kanvar sat down and leaned against his shoulder. "You're a terrific hero."

*But I was so frightened. I still am.*

"That doesn't mean you're not a hero. Heroes are always scared. They just go ahead and do what they have to anyway."

*You mean it?*

"Yes. But your father's going to kill me for dragging you into this."

*He doesn't know. There's a cave a few miles from the palace where I often go for weeks at a time while I'm writing my books. I hate to be interrupted in the middle of a scene. I left a note in my chambers saying I was going off to my cave to write and would be back when I'm done.*

"Lovely." Kanvar leaned his head back against Bensharie and closed his eyes, but images of torture and murder from the Naga's mind haunted him. Those faded into the face of Kumar Raza's brother. Rajan, alive and bound to a Great Red volcanic dragon. Kanvar shuddered and wrapped his arm across his chest. Rajan's mind had been twisted beyond any recollection of humanity. Deep down all he wanted was to hurt and kill, but he'd never do that again. By the fountain, no. Chandran had him. He would take him to the senate and execute him. Kanvar wanted to scream in frustration. Even if by some miracle he could save Rajan's body from death, his mind was already too far gone.

*Kanvar?* A cool silver presence slipped past Kanvar's brooding.

He sat up and snapped his eyes open. *Silverwave? Is that you. Yes. Just a moment.*

A few minutes later a silver serpent, scales glistening, crawled out of the ocean into the narrow rift. New scars marred her sleek sides.

"What happened?" Kanvar asked, rubbing his hand over her dragonstone in greeting.

*I was burned. The red dragon captured me and forced me to serve him, to bring his Naga to Maran, then ferry the Naga and his soldiers secretly to Daro last night. But my mind is free now. I'm not sure what happened.*

"I got Akshara's singing stone on him. He's been taken prisoner by the Maranies."

*Oh.* Silverwave rubbed her head with her webbed claws. *You do realize you can't stay in here for long. The tide will come in and drown you.*

"Yes. I know. I'm just not sure what to do. I need to talk to my grandfather. Have you seen him?"

*Last I saw he was on the docks with the dragon hunters, looking for a Naga that crashed in the water. But they were talking about killing you. Why would your grandfather do that?* Silverwave licked the scratches on Kanvar's face and hands that he'd gotten when he slid across the rocks on landing.

"He's pretending to be one of them. We went in disguise into the city to try to stop the Naga from taking over." The Naga was Rajan. Rajan alive? But not for long.

"Do you think you could get my grandfather and bring him here without the dragon hunters seeing him?"

*I can if he walks out on the docks where I can reach him.*

"Good. Let's hope he does that before the tide comes all the way in."

Kumar Raza watched the Maran armada sail away. The Varnan soldiers let them go unhindered, believing General Chandran's explanation that the only cause for the invasion was to capture the Naga. It was a good lie. One that everyone wanted to believe.

Qadim, the head of the dragon hunter jati and one of Raza's oldest friends still stood beside him, though the rest of the younger dragon hunters had accepted the fact that the second Naga had fallen to his death on the rocks, and his corpse slid beneath the ocean waves.

"It's good to have you back, Raza," Qadim said. "I didn't believe the reports from the Kundiland Colony that you'd resurfaced. Now I see they are correct. Where have you been all these years? You went off without telling anyone, and then there was all that bad business with your son-in-law turning out to be a Naga. I feared the worst, that you'd discovered him and he'd killed you on the spot, disposed of your body secretly, and we'd never see you again."

Kumar Raza ran his fingers along the smooth stalk of his crossbow and grimaced. Qadim's guess was too close to the truth for his liking. He'd rather give a different explanation and turn the subject away from Nagas. He cleared his throat. "I was lonely."

"Lonely?" Qadim turned watery gray eyes to stare at him. His hair had grown white over the years, though his muscled physique made Raza figure he still actively hunted dragons.

"My wife was dead. My daughter grown and married. I hunted more and more, but taking down dragons could not fill the emptiness in my heart or warm me on cold nights. I...left my weapons home and went on a different kind of hunt. A hunt for love." He let a sheepish smile crease his lips.

"You went in search of a wife?" Surprise sharpened Qadim's voice.

Water lapped against the docks, and the wind whipped salty spray into their faces. The scent of fish and wet wood hung in the air.

Kumar Raza laughed. "Does that surprise you so much? I am a man the same as any other. I have passions beyond shooting my crossbow."

"And did you find...love?" Qadim ran his fingers over his own crossbow as if trying to decide which he thought was better: a good hunt, or warm night back home with his own wife.

"Yes, I did, actually." Raza scanned the water and the sky for any sign of Kanvar and the gold dragon. If he was

144

the cause of their deaths, he would never forgive himself. He felt hollow inside, but that hollowness was quickly filling up with despair.

Qadim followed his gaze. "If the dragon landed somewhere, it will stay put as long as the sun shines. It knows we can't see it unless it moves."

Kumar Raza glanced at the sun where it hung at the top of its apex. So much had happened in such a short time. "That's fine. I have all day. It had to have landed right here somewhere. It's probably hiding that Naga under its wing. But I can stand and wait as long as a dragon can. Those young dragon hunters, they're too anxious, rushing here and there. You need to train them better."

"I do my best." Qadim looked sideways at Raza. "That Naga was a cripple. Looked like your grandson to me. Older, but him. Mani said she killed him, but I guess he's not dead."

Raza let out a string of curses. "How could you and the others of the jati let my poor daughter face that nest of vipers alone? I should have been here," he said in anguish. "I would have killed them all myself, and I would have made sure they were good and dead. Oh, Mani tried. I've no doubt she tried. They must have used their powers to trick her into thinking she had."

"Does that mean the other two might be alive as well?" Qadim's voice turned grave.

"If they are, I'll kill them. I'll hunt them to the ends of this world and finish them myself." Nervous sweat trickled down Kumar Raza's back. He would have preferred to avoid this conversation, but he'd known by coming back here he would have to face it, and he'd have to be convincing.

Water sloshed once more against the dock, flinging up a spray that wet Kumar Raza's boots. The restless water acted like a storm was brewing, but the sky above was clear.

"Mani isn't here," Qadim said. "She disappeared some months ago. No one saw her leave, and no one knows where she went."

"I came to see her, just to make sure she was all right, and found she wasn't. She was starving herself, blaming herself for the Naga sons she bore, though it was no fault of her own. It was my fault. Mine. Why couldn't I see what he was? Qadim, why?"

Qadim shuffled his feet and frowned. "None of us saw it. He fooled us all. But that's how Nagas are, isn't it? That's why they're so dangerous."

"Yes. I just wish my family hadn't been mixed up with them."

"Did you kill Mani then?" Qadim looked at him as if he wasn't sure if Raza were capable of putting his own child out of her misery.

"By the fountain, no. I took her home with me. I've a little place over in Kundiland. My wife has been nursing her back to health."

"So you did find love."

"Yes, I did, and I've been living a quiet happy life for some time now. Not counting my little trip to Darvat a bit ago. I'm sure you heard rumors about that. Stories of my exploits do tend to spread and grow far out of proportion."

Qadim chuckled. "I'm surprised you managed to stay out of the sunlight for so long. You must have been very careful."

Kumar Raza snorted. "I'm always careful, always ready for anything. That's why I'm still ali—" A silver coil burst from the water, wrapped around Kumar Raza leg, and jerked him off the dock. He barely had time to gasp in a breath of air before it hauled him down deep and dragged him out into the channel.

## Chapter Eleven

**Kanvar rested beside Bensharie** until Silverwave hauled a wet and spluttering Kumar Raza into the narrow cleft and uncoiled, dropping him on the rocks.

Still clutching his crossbow in his hand, Raza jumped to his feet, rubbed the water out of his eyes, and pointed it at the serpent.

"Silverwave?" Grandfather Raza moved his finger away from the trigger and lowered the weapon. "By the fountain, don't do that again without warning me. I could have hurt you."

Silverwave's laughter rippled through Kanvar's head. He drew himself up to his feet. "She says she did warn you, slapped the dock with waves twice, wet your boots. You looked down. She thought you'd seen her."

"Kanvar." Raza took a step toward Kanvar, but Bensharie whimpered and thrashed to get his body out of line of the crossbow.

"Put the crossbow down," Kanvar said, rubbing Bensharie's shoulder to reassure him. "Bensharie, you've met my grandfather before, haven't you?"

*He shot me. Twice.* Bensharie ruffled his wings and tried to make himself small enough to hide behind Kanvar.

"Grandfather—"

"I get it. I get it." He lowered the crossbow to the ground and held his hands palm outward. "I'm sorry, little one. It was an accident. The bolt was supposed to miss, but I aimed thinking you were a much bigger dragon. Please forgive me."

Bensharie curled into a ball and hid his head under his wing.

"Grandfather, this is Bensharie, Rajahansa's youngest son. He's an author and a poet and my friend."

"Rajahansa's youngest. I shot..." Raza's face went red. "I'm dead. I am so dead."

"I imagine he's going to kill both of us, just as soon as he finds out Bensharie isn't off in his cave composing some epic like he said he would be." Kanvar continued to rub Bensharie's shoulder, wishing Bensharie's identity was the only one he had to divulge to his grandfather. Perhaps he should keep the news of Rajan secret. Kumar Raza already thought his twin brother was dead. Why tell him Rajan was alive just before he would be killed again?

But Silverwave wrapped around Kumar Raza and rubbed her webbed hands over his face and hair. Then pointed to his chest and repeated the gesture. He tried to ward her off, but she persisted.

"By the fountain, Kanvar. What's she trying to say? Tell me before she smothers me."

Kanvar shuddered and pulled away from Bensharie. "Let him be, Silverwave. I'll talk to him."

*You were thinking about not telling him at all.*

*He won't take it well.*

*But they're the same. They look exactly the same. You have to tell him. Kumar Raza is my friend. He must know.*

"All right, Silverwave. Back off. I told you I'd do it."

With a hiss, Silverwave uncurled from Kumar Raza and went to sit in the ocean spray at the front of the crevice where water was already starting to crash over the rock and wash into the hole.

"She seems upset," Grandfather Raza said.

"She is." Kanvar buckled on his father's sword and rummaged through the supplies for his crossbow and harness, anything to keep from looking into his grandfather's eyes while he spoke. "So am I. The Naga I helped General Chandran capture is bound to a Great Red volcanic dragon. The dragon has twisted his mind to pure evil. I saw his thoughts. There is no humanity left in him."

*He lives in torment. We have to help him,* Silverwave prompting Kanvar to repeat her words to Raza, but Kanvar kept them to himself.

*There is nothing we can do to help*, he told her.

Kumar Raza raked his fingers through his beard. "I suppose it's for the best that we couldn't get him away from Chandran then. The general will make his death swift and painless."

Silverwave reared up on her hind legs, spread her silver wings, and hissed. She bared her fangs at Kanvar and snapped in his direction.

"Wait a minute," Kumar Raza said. "I'm the one who said that. Why snap at Kanvar?"

Kanvar limped forward and put a shaking hand on his grandfather's chest. His own heart beat sluggishly. There was no good way to tell Kumar Raza what Silverwave wanted him to.

"What is it? What's wrong?" Raza asked.

Still Kanvar hesitated.

*You tell him, or I'll tear you to shreds. I'll drag you down to the deepest part of the ocean and hold you there until your lungs explode.*

"Silverwave, please. Shut up and let me talk."

Silverwave circled Kanvar, hissing and snapping at him. Raza watched her then put a comforting hand on Kanvar's shoulder. "Whatever it is, just tell me."

Kanvar swallowed. His eyes burned with tears when he talked. "Grandfather, it's Rajan. The Naga is Rajan. He's been bound to the red dragon all these years. But there's nothing you can do for him. There is no part of Rajan left in his mind. The dragon has consumed everything. He doesn't even know his own name."

"Rajan. Rajan's alive." A surge of amazement rose up in Kumar Raza. "He's alive." The wave of hope and excitement from Kumar Raza nearly drowned Kanvar's mind. Raza's memories of his brother surged like the ocean waves. They'd done everything together, inseparable, two parts of a whole being. Days sparring with each other, slicked with sweat in the sunlight, evenings arguing over the best way to hunt dragons as they shared a bowl of rice and roasted itchekin. Their minds joined constantly, their hearts inseparable. Then Rajan had been torn away from him, leaving his heart shredded, his body nothing more than the hide of a stuffed raptor. Kumar Raza had never recovered from losing the other half of himself so long ago. Now news that his brother still lived shivered him to the core.

Kanvar shook his head. "His body is alive. His mind is gone."

Raza strode to the front of the crevice and looked out across the channel. "We have to save him."

"Grandfather, please. I've seen into his mind. There is nothing we can do. A swift death is the only way to free him from the dragon's torment." Kanvar hated the words as they spilled out of his mouth, but he knew he was right.

Anger exploded like dragon fire in Raza's mind and lashed out into Kanvar's. It caught Kanvar unshielded, unprepared, and seared across his consciousness.

Kanvar cried out and threw up a shield between himself and his grandfather.

"How dare you?" Raza thundered at him. "You think for one moment that I will stand by and let my brother be murdered again. Were you going to keep the truth about Rajan to yourself? Would you have even told me if Silverwave hadn't made you?"

"Grandfather."

Shaking with rage, Raza pushed past Kanvar and snatched up his crossbow. "As soon as it gets dark, you and Bensharie fly straight back to Kundiland. Don't fly before then. There's a dragon hunter watching at the dock, and he will see the ripples of your movement." Raza slid the crossbow into its harness on his back and snatched up the bundle of supplies. "Silverwave, swim me across the channel right now. I have to get to Wareham before they kill my brother."

"You can't fight the entire Maran army alone," Kanvar said in alarm. "They'll cut you down before you ever get near Rajan."

"Then I will die along with my brother!"

"What good will that do?" Kanvar shouted back.

Bensharie rose to his feet and came up behind Kanvar. *Tell him you and I will go fetch his brother from the Maranies.* Fear cascaded through Bensharie's mind, and the young dragon fought hard against the current to speak. *We can fly there faster, and we have a better chance of getting him out of there alive.*

"Grandfather."

"Shut up. Don't talk to me! Silverwave, let's go."

Bensharie let out a thin roar to get Kumar Raza to look back at him, then he puffed joy breath into the Great Dragon Hunter's face.

Raza's eyes went vacant and he settled to the ground with a sigh.

Silverware lunged at Bensharie, planning to sink her fangs into his neck.

"Wait." Kanvar's words alone would not have stopped the serpent, but he put a commanding power into it that brought her up short. Kanvar shuddered. It was the first time he'd ever used his powers to control another being, but it seemed necessary.

"Silverwave," he said, this time without power in his voice. "Bensharie and I are going to get Rajan. You go find a boat and bring it here for Grandfather. Take it along the channel away from the Maran warships. We'll catch up to you as soon as we have Rajan."

Silverwave settled to the ground. Her stone pulsed in gratitude. She licked Kanvar's face and then shot out of the crevice.

"Bensharie, will you move Grandfather up as far away from the water as you can. I can't lift him, and I don't know how deep it's going to get in here before Silverwave returns." Kanvar moved the bundle of supplies up to the back of the crevice while Bensharie did the same to Kumar Raza, who let himself be moved without protest. He leaned his head back against the stone and hummed a hunting song.

"You know, Bensharie. I used to think that joy breath was a stupid weapon. I was wrong. You are brilliant. Thank you. Are you sure you want to do this? We barely survived our last encounter with the Maran soldiers."

Bensharie nodded. *I think Kumar Raza is right. We should not just let Rajan die. Our fathers are powerful. Perhaps they can recover his mind and shield it from the red dragon. It is worth a try.* Bensharie lowered his head so Kanvar could climb onto his back.

"Does your wing still hurt?"

*It aches a little, but not too bad. I can fly.*

"Can you carry both me and Rajan?"

*I will do it. I have to.* Bensharie walked to the opening in the rock and launched into the air, flying straight and fast across the channel. Behind them they heard a shout and the crack of a crossbow releasing its bolt. Kanvar ducked, and the bolt whizzed over his back. By the time the dragon hunter behind them had reloaded, he and Bensharie had flown out of range.

"That was a little too close," Kanvar said.

Bensharie shivered. *I think we might see a lot more even closer before the day is out.*

The Maran coast came into view, covered with a dense pine forest. Tucked in the carpet of green at the mouth of a wide river lay Wareham, the Maran capital. Granite buildings reached skyward along wide cobblestone streets. Open markets danced with valuables from all over the world: rainbow blankets and copper pots from Darvat, fish and crab caught in the Great North Ocean, spices from Varna, dragon hides of all color and variety. Shoppers in bright clothing bustled from stall to stall seemingly oblivious to the fact that their army had invaded Daro that morning without even a declaration of war and returned again with a dangerous Naga bound for execution.

Bensharie flew into the city from the side, avoiding the Maran boats and soldiers that swarmed the docks. Kanvar could see no sign of Rajan among them.

*Where does the senate meet?* Bensharie asked.

*I'm not sure.* Kanvar had only hidden in Wareham for a short time before indenturing himself to Chandran as a means to getting to Kundiland. From his vantage point in the sky, he looked across the buildings below for something like the Varnan All Council meeting hall. There were no domed buildings with stately columns.

*If we stay in the air much longer, someone's bound to spot the ripples of my flight.*

*I know. I know. Let me think.* He scanned the ground for anything that looked different than the rows of sparkling gray houses. His eyes fell on a building set apart by a wall with green lawn and gardens beyond. It had a central square hall with five wings of offices jutting out from the sides, one for each of the Maran provinces. A hundred soldiers stood guard around the grounds and building. All of them carried crossbows ready and loaded. Several had spy glasses and were gazing across the city looking for gold dragon movement.

*Over there.* Kanvar guided Bensharie's thoughts to the complex close to the river edge of the city.

Bensharie pulled up short and circled back away, fearing the soldiers had already seen him.

*No. Don't fly harder. Just land somewhere. They can't see you if you're not moving, and I need to think.*

Bensharie dropped to the closest rooftop and froze.

*It seems Chandran doesn't believe we crashed into the rocks and died.* Kanvar rubbed his sword hilt, his mind spinning, trying to think of a way past the soldiers.

*There's so many of them. Which part of the building do you think they've got Rajan?*

*If they haven't killed him yet, I'll bet he's in that central hall.*

*It has windows I think I can fit through, but they're blocked with glass.*

Kanvar pulled out his crossbow and loaded it. *I think our best chance is to fly straight at that biggest window there on the side. Joy breath the soldiers as you pass over them and hope their bolts don't hit us before your breath hits them. I'll fire into the glass and break it. You fly through, grab Rajan and come right back out. Fly straight up so we can get out of their range the fastest. Then head for the channel to meet up with Silverwave. Rajan's wearing a singing stone. I won't be able to hear your thoughts once we get in range.*

Bensharie sucked in a deep breath and started to tremble beneath Kanvar. Intense fear kept him from speaking or moving. Kanvar felt the same fear. Their chances of succeeding weren't the best.

*We could fly back to Kundiland instead like Grandfather Raza told us to*, Kanvar offered.

Bensharie shook his head. *We told Silverwave we'd do this.* He leaped into the air, flapping hard, and flew straight for the building. The soldiers had half the length of the city to see him coming and get ready. But Bensharie put on a burst of speed and sucked in a deep breath. Kanvar readied his crossbow.

A cry of alarm went up as Bensharie came over the wall and shot above the lawn toward the big window at the side of the building. Crossbows cracked, releasing their bolts at the same moment Bensharie breathed a spurt of glittering breath at the men below.

Bensharie roared in pain as one of the bolts hit him in the shoulder, but he continued flying at full speed toward the waiting glass.

Kanvar discharged his own crossbow. It slammed into the glass, shattering the window seconds before Bensharie would have hit it. Shards of glass were still falling as they passed through into the hall. A wave of shrill pain blasted through Kanvar's mind as they came in range of the singing stone. It blinded him for a moment, and he jerked unexpectedly as Bensharie twisted and dove, then rocketed back up and out the window.

Since the sound of the singing stone stayed with them, Kanvar figured Bensharie had managed to grab Rajan by the shoulders and haul him out.

Bensharie flew hard, but the bolt in his shoulder made his flight uneven, and he leveled off low enough the soldiers could hit him again.

Gritting his teeth, Kanvar bent down and tore the crossbow bolt from Bensharie's shoulder. Bensharie bellowed in pain.

"Lick the wound!" Kanvar shouted at him.

The soldiers right below them were dazed by the joy breath, but more ran around the building to get a shot at the dragon.

Bensharie twisted his head and licked his shoulder.

"Now fly. Fly!" Kanvar cried.

Bensharie beat his wings hard and lifted further into the sky just as another round of crossbow bolts rose through the air toward him. A bolt hit one of his back legs. He cried out in pain and let go of Rajan with that claw. Rajan dangled high in the sky, held up by only one of Bensharie's claws.

Rajan let out a muffled scream, but could not reach up and hold onto Bensharie because his hands were still bound behind his back.

Bensharie stopped flying upward and dove for the channel.

Kanvar gritted his teeth and hoped Rajan wouldn't slip from his grasp until they found Silverwave and the boat. Kanvar realized too late he wouldn't be able to feel Silverwave's mind to guide him to her.

## Chapter Twelve

**Kanvar gritted his teeth** as Bensharie shot above the warships and turned eastward flying hard up the channel. But he grew tired and couldn't keep his altitude with the weight of both Kanvar and Rajan. Kanvar looked down and saw blood streaming from Rajan's shoulder Bensharie had clutched in his claw. The blood made Bensharie's grip slippery.

Heavy ballista fire cracked from the warships behind them. Kanvar knew a single one of those bolts would kill Bensharie. Water splashed to their right and ahead of them, as the first bolt missed.

"Fly. Fly!" Kanvar screamed.

Bensharie pumped his wings, but it did little to increase his speed.

The ballista fired again. This time the bolt passed through the air next to Rajan.

Rajan thrashed to avoid it and slipped from Bensharie's grasp.

He fell.

Water splashed below them, and Silverwave broke the surface, leaping high into the air. She spread her wing spines, controlling her glide so she could snatch Rajan from the air and wrap around him before diving back below the surface and speeding away. Her undulating movement brought Rajan to the surface just often enough for him to catch a necessary breath of air between dives.

Without Rajan's weight, Bensharie regained his speed. He didn't waste any effort on added altitude, but zipped straight forward, following Silverwave. The ballista fired several more times, but the bolts hit the water farther and farther behind him.

A life boat from one of the Maran warships came into view, bouncing on the water. Packed full, it would hold eight men. Only one occupied it. Kumar Raza's red dragonscale armor stood out from the muted brown of the boat and blue-green water. Two heavy whaling harpoons were lashed, one on either side of the boat, being too long to fit inside. They gave the small craft a certain oddness that bothered Kanvar.

Silverwave heaved Rajan into the boat, and Kanvar was relieved to see that Akshara's singing stone still hung around his neck. Kumar Raza eased his brother to the bottom of the boat, checked to make sure he was still breathing, and slathered his shoulder with Great dragon saliva. Then he called up to Bensharie. "Land in the water. Gently. Can you swim?"

Breathing heavily, Bensharie settled into the water. He couldn't use his hurt back leg to swim, but he spread his wings across the top to keep himself afloat.

Kanvar climbed from Bensharie's back into the boat while Silverwave dove beneath the surface, extracted the crossbow bolt from Bensharie's back leg, and licked the wound closed.

Ignoring the penetrating shriek from the singing stone with him in the boat, Kanvar reached over and rubbed Bensharie's dragonstone. "Bensharie, you were so brave. What a hero you are." He hugged Bensharie's neck, but leaning out so far almost capsized the boat.

"Steady there." Kumar Raza adjusted his position so his weight counterbalanced Kanvar's moves. He glanced back up the channel, and Kanvar followed his gaze. The Maran armada had set their sails and was headed toward them.

Kanvar's heart dropped. "We won't make it, will we? One life boat against their whole fleet."

Kumar Raza rubbed his beard. "They're sailing against the wind. At least we have that on our side. As long as we sail eastward and the wind holds, we can stay ahead of them."

"How?"

"Silverwave. That's how. But hold up a second, Silver." Grandfather Raza switched places with Kanvar and reached-ed out to Bensharie. "How are you feeling? Can you fly now if Kanvar stays in the boat?"

Bensharie pointed at the singing stone then at Kanvar.

"Right." Raza leaned down and grabbed it.

Kanvar caught his arm. "What are you doing?"

"Getting rid of it."

"No. You can't. He's too powerful."

"You're powerful too."

"Not without Dharanidhar, I'm not. Rajan is so...he can do things to people's minds I've never even dreamed of."

Grandfather let go of the singing stone. Rajan stared up at them from the bottom of the boat. A heavy gag in his mouth kept him from speaking. His arms and legs were both bound. But even with all that and the singing stone, the look in Rajan's eyes terrified Kanvar. It was cunning and cruel and seemed to say he would get free sooner or later and then he would devour them both.

A ballista cracked and the bolt hit the water just short of the life boat.

"Silverwave, get us out of here." Kumar Raza yelled. "Bensharie, fly."

Silverwave shot forward, dragging the life boat faster than any sailing vessel could go. Bensharie took to the air, keeping pace though he had not rested long enough to regain his full strength.

"We need to take Rajan to Kundiland to my father." Kanvar said above the howl of the singing stone in his mind. "Bensharie thinks Amar and Rajahansa might be strong enough to restore his mind and block him from the red dragon's."

Grandfather Raza shook his head. His face was a tight mask. His eyes smoldered. "Silverwave knows where the red dragon's lair is."

"What good will going there do?"

"I'm going to kill it."

Rajan let out a muffled shout, rolled up onto his knees, and launched himself at his brother. He almost succeeded in knocking Kumar Raza overboard, but Raza wrapped him in a bear hug and slammed him back down to the bottom of the boat.

"Hand me that rope, Kanvar."

Kanvar grabbed a rope from where it rested beside their bundle of supplies and tossed it to his Grandfather. Kumar Raza secured Rajan to the bench at the front of the boat, but Rajan continued to thrash and scream through the gag. Kumar Raza reached around to the back of his head to untie it.

"I wouldn't do that," Kanvar said. The shriek from the singing stone made him want to scream as well, but he clenched his fist and tried to ignore it.

"Why not? With the singing stone he can't use his powers even if he can talk." Kumar Raza got the gag loose and pulled it out of Rajan's mouth.

Rajan growled and bit Kumar Raza's shoulder. When he found he couldn't bite through the dragonscale armor, he went for Kumar Raza's face.

Kumar jerked back in surprise, but Rajan's teeth left a bloody scrape down his cheek and tore hair from his beard.

Rajan howled in rage. "I'm going to kill you both. Tear out your entrails, snap your bones, and feast on your flesh. We had the whole world in our hands, and you ruined it. We are so hungry, and you've cut us off from our dragon self. Useless humans. Free us now, or we will destroy you." He roared again and thrashed to free himself.

Kumar Raza put his hand to his bleeding face.

Kanvar's stomach churned, and he leaned over for a moment to keep from being sick.

Kumar Raza frowned at his brother, then spoke to Kanvar. "You weren't exaggerating."

Kanvar shook his head, then he glanced at the heavy whaling harpoons lashed to the sides of the boat. "But I don't understand. Why insist on saving him from the Maranies only to kill his dragon? Either way they both die."

Kumar Raza grimaced and ran his fingers through his beard. He stared hard at his brother for a moment then went to their bundle of supplies in the back of the boat. Without answering Kanvar, he filled a tin cup with water from a waterskin and took it to his brother.

Staying back where he wouldn't be bit, Kumar Raza held the cup up for Rajan to see. "It's water. Are you thirsty?"

Rajan stopped thrashing and glared at him.

Kumar Raza reached forward and pressed the cup to Rajan's lips. Rajan tipped his head forward and tried to lick the water from the cup with his tongue.

Kumar Raza let out a dark chuckle. "Try it like this." He moved the cup to his own mouth and took a gulp.

Rajan blinked at him. "Free us. We need to return to our dragon self. The stone hurts us."

"Rajan, I intend to free you. Believe me, I do." Kumar Raza set the cup against his brother's lips again.

Rajan made a sloppy attempt to drink the way Kumar Raza had shown him. Kanvar suspected more water sloshed down his chest than his throat.

Kanvar wet his own parched throat from the water-skin and glanced behind them. The Maran warships still followed, but had fallen behind. Bensharie flew just above. Kanvar ran his fingers along one of the cold iron harpoons. "You told me there was no way to kill a Great Red volcanic dragon."

Kumar Raza drew Kanvar with him to the back of the boat and spoke in a low voice so Rajan wouldn't hear them.

"I said *you* couldn't kill a Great Red dragon."

Kanvar tapped the harpoon. "Iron won't get through the crusted magma on the surface, and it will melt if you go for its mouth. My steel crossbow bolt didn't last a moment in that fire."

"Crossbow bolts are short. These harpoons are long and heavy. When the tip melts, the rest of the bolt keeps going if driven in fast and hard enough. But you couldn't even lift one, let alone thrust the full length of it into a red dragon."

"But why?" Kanvar persisted. "Why save your brother now, just to kill him later?" He and Bensharie had risked their lives to retrieve Rajan from the Maranies. It seemed a complete waste if Kumar Raza just wanted to take revenge against the red dragon.

Kumar Raza stood and shouted to get Bensharie's attention, then motioned for him to come down.

Bensharie dropped low so he skimmed the water beside the boat.

"You need to rest," Kumar Raza said. "I think we're far enough ahead of the Maranies you can do it now. Land behind the boat and grab on. Silverwave can pull you along with the rest of us for a while."

Bensharie wheeled around and landed behind them. Silverwave slowed for a moment so he could get hold and rest his head on the back of the boat.

"Hey Bensharie," Kumar Raza said. "Why don't you tell Kanvar about Nikeron? I'll bet you've read about him."

Bensharie grinned and nodded. His dragonstone glowed a brilliant gold.

"Sorry, I can't hear you." Kanvar pointed to the singing stone around Rajan's neck.

Bensharie jerked his head up and glanced between Rajan, Kumar Raza, and the harpoons. He shook his head, and his stone flashed signaling that he was speaking quickly and forcefully.

"Bensharie, it's no use," Kanvar said. "I don't understand you."

Bensharie scratched with a claw in the side of the boat. *Fiction. Not Real.*

"It might be real," Kumar Raza said, his voice rising. "Parmver says there might be a sliver of truth to it, and it's the best chance we have."

Bensharie pointed to Rajan than himself. He shook his head violently, then pushed off from the boat and started swimming the other way.

"Grandfather, what's going on?" Kanvar demanded.

Kumar Raza ignored him. Standing up in the boat he shouted after Bensharie. "That's not what I had in mind, Bensharie. I would never do that to you. Come back."

Bensharie kept going.

"Silverwave, stop him," Kumar Raza said.

Silverwave slipped from the harness she was using to pull the boat and swam after Bensharie. The boat rocked in her wake. When she reached Bensharie, the two dragons' stones flashed at each other as they conversed.

Kanvar turned to his grandfather. "Tell me what you are planning."

"All right. I'll tell you the best I can." Kumar Raza sat down in the back of the boat and motioned for Kanvar to join him.

Kanvar glanced at Rajan who had been quiet and still for an unnerving amount of time. Rajan stared back at him with venomous eyes.

Kumar Raza spoke in a low voice so only Kanvar could hear. "I believe the only way to free my brother from the red dragon's power is to sever the link that binds them."

Kanvar shivered. "There is no way."

"Only one. Kill the red dragon."

"Then Rajan will die."

"Not if he bonds with another dragon at the moment of the red dragon's death."

Kanvar glanced at the side of the boat where Bensharie had scratched the words. *Fiction. Not Real.* A cold wind whipped a spray of water in his face.

"Yes, I got the idea from a story, a legend, but I think maybe it could work. It's worth a try at least. And once the red dragon is dead and no longer interfering with his thoughts, you can go into his mind and erase the memories of his time with the red dragon. Wipe away the hurt, the evil, the torment. Everything, all the way back to the day we went hunting and my uncle shot him. That would restore him to what he once was, and he can start his life over again."

Kanvar's stomach—already queasy from Rajan's talk of eating people, the rocking of the boat, and the pain that lashed through his mind from the singing stone—rebelled completely. The thought of going into Rajan's mind and destroying it in such a fashion set Kanvar heaving over the side of the boat. When his stomach stopped convulsing, he wiped the sour taste from his mouth and slumped back on the bench.

Kumar Raza offered him some water, but he waved it away, not daring to put anything else inside him. He glanced out across the ocean to where Silverwave and Bensharie conversed. Sunshine reflected off the ripples and flashed in his eyes.

"You can't ask Bensharie to take Rajan's bond," he told his grandfather. "It would destroy his mind before I ever got the chance to erase Rajan's memories." Kanvar let out a bitter laugh. "Bensharie couldn't even bring himself to lick my wounds closed because they were bleeding."

"I wouldn't dare even suggest such a thing," Grandfather Raza said. "He's Rajahansa's son, for goodness sake. He's already got three nasty scars now that I have no doubt Rajahansa will make me pay dearly for."

"But he thought that's what you were trying to suggest. No wonder he swam away."

Kumar Raza threw his hands up. "I didn't mean for him to take it that like that. Silverwave has already agreed to attempt to bond with Rajan. She's fond of him, the fountain knows why with the way the red dragon made him treat her."

"Because he looks like you?"

"Yes probably. A much younger me. Though I have to say the apparent age difference is startling. I could be his father, grandfather even."

"Naga's don't age like humans."

"Don't I know it." Kumar Raza ran his hands over his face as if feeling the wrinkles that had started to form at the corners of his eyes and mouth.

Kanvar chuckled, but wondered if his own face would wrinkle early because of his bond with Dharanidhar who was already quite grandfatherly for the age of dragons.

The water splashed as Silverwave ducked below the surface and swam back to the boat. Bensharie followed, head down. He floated beside Kumar Raza and patted him on the shoulder as if to apologize, but then shot a terrified look at Rajan.

Kanvar realized in shock that Rajan had managed to chew his way through the rope that bound him to the boat and had started on the one that tied his feet.

Kumar Raza swore, went to the front of the boat, and with much cursing and fighting, and a few more bites on his face, managed to get Rajan tied back down and gagged.

"You'd think he wouldn't be able to move at all with that stone around his neck. I'm on the other side of the boat from it, and I just want to curl up and die," Kanvar said while Grandfather Raza dabbed dragon saliva on the bites.

Kumar Raza growled under his breath and motioned for Silverwave to get them moving again. Bensharie grabbed onto the back of the boat and let it pull him as the sun set behind them.

The falling darkness added to Kanvar's sense of dread. They were going to face a Great Red volcanic dragon. They could all be killed, or worse, captured. He could still not picture how even the heavy whale harpoons could penetrate the dragon's outer crust. And all for the chance, the possibly, like in some make-believe story, Rajan may be able to forge a new bond with Silverwave. Kanvar shuddered and gripped the side of the boat.

Behind them, the Maran armada strove against the wind to narrow the gap enough to once again fire their ballistae.

Rebecca Shelley

## Chapter Thirteen

**Kumar Raza squinted at** the Darvat shoreline as it approached. Silverwave had taken them the shortest distance between Maran and Darvat like he'd asked her to, knowing the waterskin he'd packed would not provide enough water for Bensharie.

Gold rippled the early morning sunlight away to the side of the boat where Bensharie flew. He'd rested, letting Silverwave pull him for most of the night. Then when the sky started to turn gray, he'd offered to fly again and carry Kanvar with him.

Kanvar's face was pale, and black circles hung under his eyes. He'd refused to eat or drink anything, and Kumar Raza could tell Akshara's singing stone was tearing his mind apart. Bensharie was right; Kanvar needed to get away from the stone. Kumar Raza had helped him onto Bensharie's back without tipping over the boat, and the two youngsters had flown off out of range of the stone. As soon as they were a safe distance, Kanvar had leaned his head on Bensharie's neck and closed his eyes. Kumar Raza feared he had fallen unconscious. But Bensharie had flown on, following Silverwave's tireless swim.

The sunlight reflecting off the water made it hard for Kumar Raza to see the Darvat shore ahead. He'd asked Silverwave to find them fresh water and hoped she could do it soon. Salt from the spraying ocean waves crusted his beard and dried his mouth with its bitter tang.

Beside him, Rajan moaned and shifted.

Kumar Raza put a comforting hand on his brother's chest, wishing he could be rid of the stone that tormented him. Rajan's eyes fluttered open for a moment then closed again. Kanvar had said Akshara's stone had nearly killed Devaj when he'd worn it for too long. It seemed to be doing the same to Rajan. Each minute, all night long, Kumar Raza had watched his brother weaken, his face become waxy, his eyes vacant. Kumar Raza could hear the stone's song, but it was faint and far away in his mind. He had Naga blood in him, yes, but he was not a real Naga. The stone could not hurt him like it was doing to Kanvar and Rajan.

Glancing at the ripple that marked Bensharie and Kanvar's flight and hoping Kanvar wouldn't notice, Kumar Raza lifted the glowing purple crystal from his brother's chest and looped the chain with its deadly stone over his own head. It settled against his armor, the purple glow clashing against his red dragonscales like a ghostly specter. When he rubbed the stone, it sent shivers through him. Usually where there was light, there was heat, but this stone seemed to suck the warmth from his hand and siphon it down from his arm.

He pulled his hand away and went to sit at the back of the boat as far from his brother as he could get.

Rajan opened his eyes and looked around. It took several minutes for him to focus on Kumar Raza. A tinge of color returned to his face. He growled something through the gag, but Kumar couldn't make out what he said.

"I'm sorry, Rajan. I can't have you chewing through the ropes or trying to bite me, otherwise I'd ungag you right now." He wished he could. He wanted to talk to his brother. Needed to find some way to connect with the part of Rajan that had once been good, the part that had watched over and protected Kumar Raza when they were young.

"Do you know who I am?" he asked Rajan.

Rajan howled something through the gag that sounded like father and murderer.

Kumar Raza raked his fingers through his beard. "Yes, I know I look like our father, but I'm not. I'm Kumar. Your brother, Kumar. And I'm trying to help you."

Rajan thrashed against his bonds.

"Stop, please. You're hurting yourself." Kumar Raza imagined the tight ropes cutting into his own flesh. At one time, he and his brother had shared every physical sensation. If he stubbed his toe, Rajan had felt it. If Rajan nicked himself while practicing with his sword, Kumar Raza experienced the pain along with him. Their bond had once been almost as deep as the bond between Naga and dragon. As twins they had lived their life as one. Kumar had not realized how tightly they'd been intertwined until his link with his brother had been severed on the day he thought their father had killed him. From that moment on, Kumar Raza had felt himself only half a man. There was an emptiness in his soul that could not be filled by any food, drink, or physical pursuit. He had lived with the constant ache for decade after decade. It was that pain that had fueled his desperate search for the Great Gold dragons, that pain that had caused him to swear never to kill his own offspring if they were Nagas, that pain that allowed him to celebrate his daughter's marriage to the Naga King. Kumar Raza's whole life and destiny had been forged in that one moment of horror when his brother had been murdered.

And now Rajan slumped in front of him only a boat length away. Alive. But Kumar Raza couldn't feel him. The singing stone kept their spirits severed. He wished he could fling the stone as far as he could out into the water. Be rid of it and done, but he couldn't. His brother's bond with him had been replaced by a bond with the most cruel and bloodthirsty of beings. The Great Red volcanic dragon. A monster who, not only preferred human flesh above all other food, but also captured humans and kept them alive to torture and breed. Kumar Raza had killed two Great Red dragons before, and the horror of seeing the condition of the people he'd freed would never be washed from his mind. The thought that his brother had been such a prisoner for so long repulsed him. Worse than just a physical prisoner, the Great Red dragon had taken over Rajan's mind as well.

Kumar Raza shook his head, but the images would not go away. "Rajan, I'm your brother." He tried once more to reach out to his twin.

Rajan growled and tried to tear free. His fingers clawed at the ropes and bench until his nails broke and bled.

Kumar Raza thought about putting the singing stone back on him. At least that had kept him still. Too still. Deathly still. Raza couldn't risk it killing his brother before they reached the red dragon's island. But that would be days away. They would have to follow the coast of Darvat around to the eastern side, and then cross more open water to reach the Eastern Isles, a maze of volcanic islands no explorer had ever charted completely. Somewhere among those islands the Great Red dragon waited, and when Kumar Raza found it, he would end his brother's torment one way or another.

He patted the closest harpoon. "Don't worry, Rajan. I *will* free you. Your pain will end."

Somewhere behind them just at the edge of the horizon the Maran war fleet still followed.

Kanvar's heart dropped as a plume of hot ash came into view on the horizon. *It's a volcano*, he said in alarm to Bensharie. Over the past few days, flying with Bensharie had begun to feel natural to Kanvar. They had flown during the day, cooked their meals, ate, drank, and rested on shore at night, and followed Silverwave. But their rests had been short. The Maran ships hounded them.

When Kanvar reached out with his mind, he could feel General Chandran's determination to hunt Rajan to the end of the world if necessary. Rajan had deprived Chandran's countrymen of their most prized possession, their freedom, a possession that was Chandran's sworn duty to protect. Kanvar chuckled, he would have bet the Maranies' most prized possession was money, since they cared little for the freedom of anyone else as long as they made a profit off them.

*Of course it's a volcano*, Bensharie said. *Where else would a Great Red volcanic dragon live?*

Despite the cool ocean wind, Kanvar's face stung with the memory of the burns he'd gotten trying to rescue his grandfather, Frost, and Denali from the volcano that had erupted in the Great North. *I hate volcanoes.*

Bensharie dipped his wings so Kanvar could see the boat where his grandfather sped through the water toward the island below the erupting cloud of ash and magma. *How do you suppose he plans to kill the red dragon*, Bensharie mused.

*I don't know, but I can't see how he can do it and keep Rajan alive when the wound appears on the Naga's body at the same instant it does on the dragon's. Let's say he does somehow, don't ask me how, get one of those harpoons through the crust of black rock over the dragon, through its scales, and into its heart. The wound would kill Rajan instantly. There will be no time for him to bond with Silverwave.*

*Perhaps he intends to kill the red dragon slowly.* Bensharie shuddered.

Kanvar patted Bensharie's shoulder. *But if he doesn't strike fast and true, the dragon will devour him before he gets a second strike.*

As they drew closer to the island, they saw a string of tall cinder cones with wisps of smoke rising from each as if they were half-dormant, except for the last which thundered and raged while it spewed its contents into the sky. Lava flowed down its slopes and sizzled into the pounding waves, sending up a curtain of steam. Lush vegetation grew around the base of the dormant cones and white sandy beaches glittered in the sun. The rising mist cooled and let fall a fine spray of raindrops. A rainbow lit the air.

*That is frighteningly beautiful,* Bensharie said. *I wish I had my quill and paper here. Just the sight of it screams for a poem.*

*We're about to fight a Great Red dragon, and you're thinking poetry?* Kanvar ran his hand along his crossbow, checking to make sure it and the bolts were secure on his back. Then he felt for his hunting knife and his father's sword. The hunting knife was gone, taken by the Maran soldiers, but the sword and crossbow were still in place. *Do you suppose it suspects we're coming? Do you think it can feel the singing stone?*

*A rainbow dream, drenched in steam, fire at its heart. Death the mountain rumbled. Death the dragon roared.*

*Shut up,* Kanvar said.

Bensharie fell silent for a moment then said, *I can't wait to get home and write this down.*

*It would be nice to get home at all,* Kanvar grumbled. *But the odds of our surviving aren't very good.*

Below them, Silverwave reached the shore, pulled the boat up onto the beach, and dragged it into the deep vegetation where it couldn't be seen. Bensharie flared his wings and landed on the white sand. The mist condensed on Kanvar's blue armor as he slid off Bensharie's back and headed into the trees. His stomach recoiled at going anywhere near the singing stone, but he pushed leafy fronds out of his way and joined his grandfather and Silverwave by the boat.

"Did you sense where the red dragon is as you flew up?" Grandfather asked Kanvar as he unlashed the harpoons from the side of the boat.

"No. I had my shields up. I don't want my mind anywhere near that monster. He'd suck me in and tear me apart." Kanvar looked over to the boat where Rajan was still bound. His wrists and ankles were swollen and raw from the tight ropes. His eyes burned into Kanvar like live coals, and the singing stone was gone from his chest.

Kanvar shrunk back, surprised. The singing stone's voice pounded his mind with its song. It had to be here. "Grandfather," Kanvar said in alarm.

Kumar Raza straightened and turned toward. The stone glowed a sickening purple against his chest.

"You took the singing stone off him?"

"It was killing him." Kumar Raza set the harpoons on the ground, pulled Kanvar's helmet from their supply bundle, and tossed it to him. "Put that on. Remember to avert your eyes when he blows fire at you. Leave your crossbow here so it doesn't get burned to a cinder. It will be useless against him."

"You're going to let me help you fight the dragon?" Kanvar pulled the helmet over his head and unbuckled the crossbow harness.

"It's the only way this might work, but you and Bensharie are going to have to do exactly what I say." Kumar Raza put on his own helmet.

"Bensharie too?"

Kumar Raza nodded. "I'd be worried that Rajahansa will kill me if anything happens to him, but if this doesn't work we'll already be dead anyway."

"You're instilling great confidence in me, Grandfather."

Kumar Raza laughed. It was the kind of dark laugh that so often erupted from Dharanidhar. Kanvar's heart twinged. For days he'd been feeling for Dharanidhar's mind, but his friend remained unconscious. Parmver's plans to nurse him back to health depended on him waking and taking the medication Parmver prepared for him. But if Dharanidhar never woke…

"Kanvar." Kumar Raza's firm hand on his shoulder made him jump. "I need to borrow your sword."

Kumar Raza reached for the sword at Kanvar's side, but Kanvar twisted out of his reach. "You don't want to do that."

Grandfather Raza scowled. "Kanvar, the sword is part of the bonding ceremony. I need it."

"All right. Go ahead." Kanvar spread his hand and turned so his grandfather could grab the hilt, but when Kumar Raza's hand closed around it, a shock of gold power flung him back into the thick leaves.

Kanvar shook his head as his grandfather picked himself up and dusted his armor off.

"Only blood from the royal Naga line can touch it," Kanvar said. "I did try to warn you."

Kumar Raza grunted in annoyance, grabbed the tin water cup from the boat, and motioned for Kanvar to join him and Silverwave next to Rajan.

Silverwave's long snake-like body was curled around the boat. She had her neck draped over the side and was licking Rajan's wrists. She raised her head and moved her coils out of the way as Kanvar limped over and climbed into the boat.

Rajan growled through his gag and tried to snap at Kanvar.

Kumar Raza pressed a firm hand against Rajan's chest to force him still. "Rajan, listen to me. You are a Naga. That is why our father tried to kill you. You are a Naga and you must bond with a Great dragon or you will die."

Rajan shook his head and continued growling.

Kanvar shuddered, but Kumar went on speaking. "This is Silverwave. You know her. She's been with you for some time now. She has agreed to bond with you. Will you let her be your dragon?"

Rajan fell silent and let out a strangled sob. *We are red dragon. We are burning.* Rajan's cry of despair went so deep Kanvar sensed it intertwined in the tortured voice of the singing stone. He recoiled and fell out of the boat, landing on his back hard enough to knock the wind out of him.

Kumar Raza leaned over the side and looked down at him. "What was that?"

Kanvar gasped until he got enough air into his lungs to speak. "Put the singing stone back on him. He's too powerful. If he can speak so I can hear him, his dragon will hear him too. He can give away our presence."

Kumar Raza's face wrinkled in a deep frown. Reluctantly he returned the singing stone to his brother's chest.

Rajan screamed and thrashed, but the gag muffled his yells and he fell back limp and silent.

"Did he say he was willing to bond with Silverwave?"

Kanvar dragged himself to his feet. "No. He said he's already bound to the red dragon."

"Well, we're going to change that." Kumar Raza grabbed Kanvar and lifted him into the boat. "You have the sword. Since it's so finicky, you use it. Are you ready, Silverwave? Hold your foreclaw out. This will hurt, but you can lick the wound closed in just a moment."

Kanvar drew his father's sword and looked over his shoulder to make sure Bensharie had not followed him to the boat. "Bensharie hates blood," he muttered. "Good thing he didn't have to try bonding with me."

"Just do it." Kumar Raza grabbed Silverwave's forearm and twisted it so her wrist faced Kanvar. With his other hand, he held the tin cup ready.

"Are you all right with this, Silverwave?" Kanvar asked. "You don't have to do this. No one can make you. Not even grandfather. The bond should be given freely."

Silverwave pointed to herself with her other hand and nodded. Then she pointed to Rajan with a questioning look.

"He has no free will to give," Kumar Raza said bitterly. "We force this bond on him, or he will die. We can only hope when his mind is once again his own, he will be happy with it."

Rajan stared at them, but his eyes had glazed over.

Kanvar's heart constricted. Every part of this was wrong. His father and Rajahansa would not approve. But then when had they approved of anything he had done? Taking a deep breath, he nicked Silverwave's wrist with the sword. Her blood flood like sea water into the cup. When it was half full, Kumar Raza released her arm, and she licked the wound closed.

Kanvar wiped her blood from the blade with the cloth and moved over to Rajan.

Rajan stared at him glassy eyed. His wrists were tied tight behind his back and secured to the bench at the front of the boat.

"I can't reach his wrists," Kanvar said.

"Does it matter where?"

Kanvar glanced down at his own leg where the sword had first cut him, simultaneously cutting Dharanidhar's hand, mixing their two bloods in the wound to create their initial link. "I guess not."

The memory of his father's admonition drifted through his mind. *It's a ceremony, Kanvar. It should be done the right way.* He shook the thought out of his mind and waited while Kumar Raza rolled up Rajan's sleeve so Kanvar could reach his upper arm.

"Rajan. This will only hurt for a moment." Kumar Raza said, gripping his brother's arm so he couldn't thrash away, but Rajan made no response.

"He probably won't feel it at all next to the pain of the singing stone," Kanvar said. He cut Rajan's arm and watched as Kumar Raza added Rajan's blood to Silverwave's in the cup, then nodded for Silverwave to close the wound.

"Do you plan to have them drink it right now?" Kanvar asked. He'd never read the story of Nikeron and wasn't sure how this was supposed to work even in a fictional way.

"No." Kumar Raza handed the cup to Silverwave along with his hunting knife. He rubbed the sparkling silver stone on her forehead. "All right, Silver, this is what you need to do, and you won't have long to do it. As soon as the first wound appears on his body, cut the gag from his mouth and make him drink half of this. You drink the other half quickly and lick the wound closed. Lick anything that bleeds. Get the singing stone off him and dump it in here." Raza pulled the cook pot and lid he'd been using to cook their food from the bundle of supplies. With a start, Kanvar realized it was made of iron.

"It's up to you to keep Rajan alive," Kumar Raza told Silverwave. "We can only hope that when I make the final strike, he will be bound to you and severed from the red dragon, because if he's not, there will be nothing you can do."

Silverwave whimpered.

"I know," Kumar Raza said. "I'm sorry. This is crazy. It's so easy for a storyteller to make things up in the safety of a warm house sitting by the fireside. It's another thing for us to try and make it real. Have you changed your mind?"

Silverwave's hand trembled on the tin cup, but she shook her head, no.

"All right." Kumar Raza lifted Kanvar out of the boat and jumped to the ground beside him.

"I can climb out of a boat myself, you know," Kanvar said, sheathing the sword. He felt naked without his crossbow on his back, but he'd rather go without it than lose it forever.

"Of course you can." Kumar Raza removed his own crossbow harness and hoisted the harpoons up on either shoulder. "Let's go hunt this cursed dragon."

## Chapter Fourteen

**Devaj ran his finger** along the dusty stone desk in the secluded cave. *Bensharie's not here, your Majesty,* Devaj sent his thoughts back to Rajahansa in the palace. *He hasn't been for a long time. There are no papers. No ink. No pens.*

Rajahansa roared and spread his mind out to connect with all the gold dragons and Nagas. *Where is Bensharie? Who saw him last?*

Thoughts tumbled as everyone collectively tried to pinpoint Bensharie's location. In the end, they found that Parmver had spoken to him last. Parmver had taken medicine to Dharanidhar and been trying to wake him when Bensharie flew into the chamber. The young gold dragon had been surprised and agitated to find Dharanidhar in the palace.

*He went alone? He went alone?* Bensharie had kept repeating as he launched himself out the window. It was a few hours after that his father found Bensharie's note saying he was going away to write.

A solemn fear gripped the dragons and Nagas as it sank in that Bensharie must have followed Kanvar to Maran.

Devaj gritted his teeth and mounted Elkatran. *I'll go after him.*

*No.* Rajahansa's command was forceful enough it bordered on compulsion. *We cannot afford to lose you too. One by one they will lure us out and kill us. Now they know we exist, we are doomed. Raahi should never have been allowed to leave the jungle village.*

*Or be taken there in the first place,* Haidar added.

Devaj sensed the undertow of thoughts from the older Nagas. This was Kanvar's fault. Kanvar had flaunted their customs, rejected the dragons Rajahansa had chosen for him, betrayed the other Nagas in bonding with their ancient enemy, endangering all their lives, and now led Rajahansa's youngest son to his death.

Devaj shook his head. It was like a nightmare he couldn't wake from.

*Traitor.*

*Outlaw.*

*Banish.*

Devaj tore his mind away from the other Nagas only to encounter a darker more powerful presence as he freed his mind from his father's shields.

*Devaj, come to me. Come. Glory awaits you and power beyond your understanding,* Khalid said.

*But my brother,* Devaj answered.

*I can save your brother.* The voice left no doubts. No arguments. Devaj knew he must return to Stonefountain.

*Father!* Elkatran screamed to Rajahansa. *Help us!*

Rajahansa's presence spread through Devaj like the golden sun across the morning sky and clashed up against Khalid's darkness.

Khalid laughed. *Greetings, Your Majesty, we have much to discuss.*

As soon as Kanvar and his grandfather cleared the range of the singing stone on their way back to Bensharie, Kumar Raza stopped. "Can you sense the red dragon, Kanvar?"

Kanvar shook his head. He'd thrown his shields back up full force as he left the singing stone behind. "I told you, we can't risk it. If I find his mind, he'll sense mine and know we're here."

"All right. I guess we do this the harder way." Kumar Raza closed his eyes and went very still. The he turned gradually to face the cinder cones, inch by inch until he was lined up with the cone closest to the active volcano. He opened his eyes. "He's up there. I can feel his rage. Being cut off from his Naga has driven him to senseless violence.

190

He screams and tears at the rocks. But he'll wear himself out soon. I'm going to need Bensharie to fly me up there first, then come back and get you."

*Bensharie*, Kanvar whispered into his friend's mind. After landing, Bensharie had frozen in place instinctively not moving so he would be invisible in the sunlight.

*He's here*, Bensharie said. *I can hear the red dragon bellowing in my mind.*

*Shield your thoughts from him, Bensharie.*

*I'm trying to, but he's so powerful.*

*You need to fly Grandfather up to the opening in his lair, then come back and get me.*

The air rippled as Bensharie flapped over. Kumar Raza eased onto his back, seeming like a giant on the small dragon. The weight of the iron harpoons made it hard for Bensharie to leap up from the sand, and once he managed it, his flight path wobbled. Kanvar watched him disappear over the trees toward the cinder cone with dread in his heart. A warning voice inside him kept insisting that they were flying off to their death. But a while later Bensharie returned.

He flopped on the sand beside Kanvar and gasped to catch his breath. *Kumar Raza is the biggest, heaviest human I've ever carried.*

"How many humans have you carried?" Kanvar asked with a laugh. "Only three of us, I'd guess: Grandfather, Rajan, and me."

*That's not the point.* Bensharie staggered to his feet and shook his head.

191

"I know." Kanvar patted Bensharie's shoulder. "Where did you leave him?"

*Outside a great big hole in the rock. That dragon must be huge. As big as Dharanidhar I'd guess. But Kumar Raza said he'd wait for us there. Are you ready?* Bensharie leaned down so Kanvar could climb onto his back.

"No. Are you?" Kanvar slid onto Bensharie and rubbed his shoulder.

*Ready to face a Great Red volcanic dragon? I'll never be ready for that. Please tell me more of that stuff about heroes being afraid and doing dangerous things anyway.*

"I will if you recite The Farmer and the Dragon poem for me again. *Oh, cowardly courage.*" Kanvar rubbed his shaking hand along his sword hilt. The blue dragonscale gauntlet rasped against the metal.

*Dear death to die in glory.* Bensharie flung himself into the air.

Kanvar's heart fluttered with every flap of Bensharie's wings. Mist peppered his face with cold drops of water. Breath rushed into his lungs and out. So alive, so close to death. His heart beat in his chest and echoed back in the veins of his arms and legs. Blood rushed through his head, making him giddy with fear. And he flew. Flew as sweet and smooth as only a Great Gold dragon can fly.

He landed almost in a trance, too aware of how fragile and valuable his own life seemed to him.

*Such thoughts*, Bensharie whispered. *You're not such a bad poet yourself.*

Kanvar flushed.

They'd landed on a rocky outcropping high up near the top of the cinder cone just outside an immense cave. Lava seeped from the rock beside them, welling into molten bubbles that dripped sluggishly down the slope. The smell of sulfur and superheated rock made Kanvar gag.

Bensharie had not exaggerated the size of the entrance to the dragon's lair, and from the long grooves scratched into the sides, the red dragon's body barely fit through the opening.

The harpoons leaned against the rock near the cave entrance, but Kanvar could not see his grandfather anywhere. His heart skipped a beat, fearing the dragon had already gotten him.

A rock near the opening moved. Kanvar blinked, the rock looked almost human, but only while it was moving. When it stopped, it blended in with the other volcanic rock around it.

"Grandfather?" Kanvar whispered.

The rock moved again, and a stone hand pressed across his mouth. "Quiet. I'm right here. I dipped myself into the magma and let it cool. I need to be invisible to the dragon."

Kanvar shuddered. He didn't want to go anywhere near the burning rock, even with his dragonscale armor.

"You don't have to." Kumar Raza must have sensed his fear. "Though that will be little consolation. Your part in this is the most dangerous." Kanvar listened with terrified amazement as his grandfather spelled out the plan for destroying the Great Red dragon.

The worst part was waiting.

His grandfather neither fidgeted nor spoke for one hour than two as the dragon raged around in its lair. They could hear roaring, scraping, and rocks crashing. Once they heard a human scream, but it fell silent before Kanvar could take a step into the cave.

His grandfather's rock-hard arm blocked his path. "Not yet. It's too late for that person anyway. There may be others we can save if we do this right. Patience, Kanvar. Wait."

Kanvar stepped back, his hand balled into a fist. He trusted his grandfather, but every moment the fear wrapped tighter and tighter around his chest.

The cave grew silent, and still they waited.

Finally, Kumar Raza tapped Kanvar on the shoulder, picked up the harpoons and disappeared into the cave. Bensharie followed him, claws clicking softly on the rock.

Kanvar gritted his teeth and waited, five minutes, ten, like he'd been told to.

Then he squared his shoulders, took a deep breath, and limped into the cave. The pock-marked volcanic stone was rough, making it difficult to place his good foot forward and find support enough to drag his crippled left leg up behind. He steadied himself against the wall and kept moving, each step a slow agony. Perhaps he shouldn't have waited so long. Had his grandfather planned for the extra time it took him to get from the entrance into the main chamber? He did not know.

An intense heat grew and thickened as he made his way through the passage. When he reached the end, he found it opened up into a vast chamber, much like his grandfather had described it would be. A pool of molten magma bubbled at its center. A raised layer of volcanic stone jutted out from the lava pool. Kumar Raza said it had been created by years and years of molten rock dripping from the red dragon as it climbed out of the magma.

Kanvar scanned the chamber for the dragon, but did not see it though there were clear signs the dragon had been there not long before. Gashes had been scrapped in the walls, and fallen stones littered the ground. Blood streaks marred the rocks. In a niche near the far edge, a stand mirror was chopped in half, the glass shattered around its base.

Even with the intense glow from the magma, Kanvar could not see his grandfather.

It took him a long moment of searching to make out the soot-covered form of Bensharie up against the wall beyond where the great rock jutted up from the ground.

A giant bubble of lava rose to the surface and burst, splattering the rock around the pool. Kanvar twisted his face away just in time for it to hit his helmet and not his eyes. His heart constricted, knowing his fear had kept him frozen in place for too long.

He forced his body to move, step, limp, step, limp over to the rock. Climbing it was difficult, his twisted leg and useless foot and his half-sized left arm barely did more than steady him as he hauled himself up with his right hand.

Near the top he slipped and almost fell back down, but the rock reached out and grabbed him. Grandfather Raza pulled him the rest of the way up then lay back down and became invisible once again.

Kanvar stood and limped toward the superheated pool. The air grew so thick and hot it seared his lips and lungs. Still, he moved forward until he stood right on the edge overlooking the lava.

More bubbles burst.

He averted his face and then turned back. Drawing his father's sword, he shouted with his mind and voice. *"Come forth, abomination, and meet your doom!"*

The red dragon's mind exploded into his own, and it recognized Kanvar as the person who had unleashed Akshara's singing stone on it.

Kanvar limped backward away from the edge, putting as much distance as he could between himself and the magma.

The dragon roared as it burst out of the lava pool. Its body glowed molten red. Lava dripped from its scales as it climbed onto the rock.

Kanvar gasped. The monster made the lesser volcanic dragon he had faced in Kundiland seem like a child's toy.

The Great Red dragon spread its wings, roared so loud the mountain shook, and blew a ball of fire at Kanvar.

Rebecca Shelley

Kanvar turned his back and let the flames wash over him. After they dissipated, he faced the dragon once more and raised his father's sword so the dragon could see it. "I am Kanvar, son of Amar, the grandson of King Khalid, heir to the golden throne, ruler of the world. All humans and dragons are under his sovereignty. You have broken his law by forcing a bond with a helpless Naga, invading the human lands, and attempting conquest and subjugation of the world and usurpation of his throne. King Amar's judgment is upon you, and he has sent me to strike you down."

*The Great Gold King has sent you?* The red dragon laughed in derision and stepped toward Kanvar. *A crippled child? Does he think so little of me? I Erebus the Devourer, the most powerful dragon in the world, destroyer of men and dragons, blaster of villages, master of Naga power.* The red dragon's mind crashed into Kanvar's with the impact of a volcanic blast.

Kanvar screamed as the dragon's consciousness burned through his own. He was powerless to stop the force of the attack.

The Great Red dragon rose up on his hind legs and flared his wings. *Kneel to me you worthless lump of coal.*

The dragon's compulsion forced Kanvar to his knees.

Kanvar struggled to wrench his mind and body back under his own control. If he failed to move according to plan, all would be lost.

The red dragon raked claws of torment through Kanvar's consciousness. The searing pain snapped Dharanidhar

197

awake. After so long, Kanvar felt the Great Blue dragon shudder and rise.

*Kanvar?* Dharanidhar said. His voice was faint from the distance and fuzzy from unconsciousness. *Where are you? What are you doing?*

*Trying to fight a Great Red volcanic dragon here. I could really use your help.* Kanvar let Dharanidhar see a picture of the burning monster that towered over him and had seized control of his mind.

Dharanidhar let out an angry roar and flung the red dragon's presence from Kanvar's mind.

Kanvar limped to his feet and raced toward the edge of the rock.

A burning claw wrapped around him and lifted him into the air.

Kanvar swung the sword at the back of the dragon's hand. It flared gold as it cut through the molten claw.

Roaring in pain, the dragon dropped Kanvar over the edge of the rock.

Kanvar screamed.

Bensharie launched out of hiding, caught Kanvar, and set him down on the floor of the cavern far enough away from the red dragon it would have to come down off its rock to reach him.

"Is that the best you can do?" Kanvar yelled. "I have the sword of the king. No armor or dragonscale can stop it. It always strikes true."

The red dragon sucked in a breath and then blew out a long stream of fire at Kanvar.

Bensharie took flight to avoid the fire. Kanvar held his ground, turning so the flames licked his dragonscale armor. Sweat slicked his skin beneath the armor, and the heat made him dizzy. While his back was turned, the red dragon launched himself from the rock at Kanvar, intending to snap him up in his jaws.

At the last moment, Kanvar jumped to the side and swung the sword at the dragon's face, slicing a deep gouge across its right cheek.

The dragon shook its head and snapped again. Kanvar had to drop flat to keep from being caught in its jaws.

Bensharie roared and flew at its face, clawing at its eyes. Stone crackled as the lava on the dragon's scales started to cool and solidify. They were running out of time.

*Not the eyes,* Kanvar thought to Bensharie, picturing Rajan blind for the rest of his life, but Bensharie couldn't get close enough to get his claws in.

With Bensharie flapping around his face, the red dragon left off attacking Kanvar and went after the young gold dragon.

Bensharie retreated back toward the high rock. The red dragon lumbered after him, breathing a hot fire that would have melted Bensharie's golden scales if Bensharie hadn't twisted away at the last second. Just as the red dragon came even with the rock, Bensharie did a flip in the air, came down at the red dragon from straight above, and let out a blast of joy breath in his face. It was a pitifully small amount of sparkling breath.

Kanvar jumped to his feet and readied his sword, afraid it wouldn't be enough to affect the red dragon.

The Great Red dragon shook his head and roared, but its roar broke into a scream of pain as Kumar Raza rose to his feet atop the rock and drove the first harpoon into its chest. The magma on the dragon had not cooled to solid rock yet, and the sharp iron spike drove past magma and scale and fiery flesh, melting as it went in. But Kumar Raza kept driving it straight into the dragon until his gauntlet-protected hands came right up against the dragon's burning body. The speed and force of the blow, though it did not kill the dragon, did enough damage that the dragon stumbled against the rock, lowered its head to look at the wound, and let out a cry of pain.

Kanvar watched transfixed as Kumar Raza snatched up the second harpoon and drove it through the red dragon's eye into its brain.

The dragon convulsed, tearing at the rock, rending out great chunks of volcanic stone.

Kumar Raza leaped from the high rock down the back side, putting it between himself and the thrashing dragon.

Bensharie snatched Kanvar out of the way as the red dragon slammed to the ground where Kanvar had been standing and went still. Rock crackled as its body cooled to black stone.

Kanvar felt the dragon's spirit tear free from its body and slip away. Like with the death of the other Great dragons he'd been a part of, Kanvar felt the shock of emptiness at the dragon's passing. He gasped and sheathed his father's sword.

"Bensharie," Kumar Raza raced around the stone and the fallen dragon. "Take Kanvar to Rajan. Kanvar, you know what you have to do."

Kanvar shuddered. His grandfather wanted him to do damage to Rajan's already tormented mind. Erase everything, all his life, all his memories clear back to his childhood.

Bensharie set Kanvar down and knelt so Kanvar could climb up on his back, but Kanvar hesitated. "I don't think I can do it."

His grandfather, still incased in the thin rock covering over his armor, lumbered up to him. "I'm begging you to do this, Kanvar. Please. I need my brother back."

"Assuming he's still alive."

Kumar Raza pressed his hand over his heart. "I can't feel him, but he's been gone from me for so long it might not mean anything. Please, Kanvar. If you have any love for me, go to Rajan. Do what you can for him?"

"I'll try, Grandfather." Feeling sick, Kanvar climbed onto Bensharie's back. "I'll send Bensharie back up for you as soon as we land."

Kumar Raza shook his head. "There are people locked in these caves that need my help. Just wait on the beach for me to join you." A haunted look lingered in his eyes.

With a sinking feeling, Kanvar realized that Kumar Raza was afraid to go down to the beach and find his brother dead, struck down by his own hand. "I'll come find you when I've done what I can for Rajan," Kanvar told him.

"Thank you." Kumar Raza patted Bensharie's shoulder, and the gold dragon took to the air and zipped out of the cave.

## Chapter Fifteen

**Bensharie landed on the** sand, and Kanvar slid from his back. The smell of wet greenery eased the scent of sulfur and molten rock that clung to Kanvar. A breeze ruffled the palm fronds and tickled his sweat-streaked face. Behind him, the ocean waves lapped at the shore, sizzling with foam as they sucked back off the sand.

Kanvar licked the salty sweat from his lips and limped toward the place where Silverwave had drawn the lifeboat into the foliage.

Bensharie followed. *Can you feel him?*

"The singing stone is silent, but I can't sense Rajan yet."

Bensharie shook his head sadly, and his gold dragon-stone flashed in the sunlight. Shadows dappled the ground as Kanvar pushed through the plants. The boat came into view with Rajan still tied to the bench, unmoving, his head slumped forward. Blood covered his chest. Silverwave lay beside the boat, shaking.

Kanvar rushed to the boat and climbed in. So much blood. Bensharie whimpered and backed out of the trees, returning to the beach.

Kanvar tore off his gauntlets, grabbed a cloth from the supplies, and wiped the blood away. A livid four-inch circular scar stood out on Rajan's chest. Silverwave had licked the wound closed.

Fearing what he would see, Kanvar tilted Rajan's head back to look at his face. A bright scar ran across his right cheek, but his eye and skull were intact.

Rajan exhaled a faint breath, then inhaled a trickle of air.

Kanvar's eyes stung. *He's alive*, he called to his grandfather. *Unconscious, but alive.* Kumar Raza could not hear Kanvar's words in his mind, but he could understand the meaning. Kanvar sensed his relief and a blossom of joy.

Silverwave whimpered, and Kanvar turned his attention to her. In shock, he realized she had scars to match Rajan's on her chest and face. Kanvar checked their hands for the cut he'd given the red dragon. Rajan's hand was scarred, but Silverwave's was not. Of course, because grandfather had told her to drink the blood as soon as she saw the first cut.

"Silverwave." Kanvar ran a calming hand down her side. "It's all right. Everything is all right now." But she continued to shake. Her eyes were closed and her mind shielded from him.

"Silverwave, what's wrong? Let me help you." He gently rubbed her dragonstone.

She whimpered again and pressed her foreclaws against her head. Her shields let down, and Kanvar felt a stabbing pain inside her skull. His stomach roiled. Kumar Raza's last strike to the red dragon had not physically manifest to Rajan and Silverwave like the other wounds had, but both serpent and Naga had felt it.

"So sorry," Kanvar said. "So, so sorry. I don't think Grandfather realized you would be wounded as well." Concentrating, Kanvar rested his hand against her forehead and tried to produce a wave of golden power to ease the pain and sooth her mind, like Devaj and Parmver had done for him several times. At first the power flickered. Parmver had not taught him this skill, Kanvar could only imitate what he'd seen done. Taking a deep breath, he relaxed his mind and tried again, concentrating on soothing the pain and comforting the stricken silver serpent. He got a headache from the attempt, but Silverwave stopped shaking. She licked his face, and Kanvar pulled his hand away.

"Better?"

*Yes. Thank you.* Silverwave rubbed Rajan's chest and face with her webbed claw. *I can't feel his mind now.*

"He's unconscious. His mind is not awake, so you can't feel it. But don't panic. I'm going to see what I can do for him next." Kanvar rubbed his headache away and was grateful to have the feel of Dharanidhar's thoughts back in his own mind. The Great Blue dragon was speaking to

Parmver who had brought him some medicine. They were arguing about how awful it tasted.

Kanvar stifled a laugh.

Kanvar's father walked into Dharanidhar's chambers and surveyed the dragon. "You're awake. Good. Where's Kanvar? I'm assuming he's alive since you are."

Dharanidhar rumbled a greeting to Amar and said, *Kanvar, Kumar Raza, and Bensharie have just succeeded in killing a Great Red volcanic dragon.*

"What?" Amar's shock and amazement pounded through Kanvar's link with Dharanidhar.

*I'm fine.* Kanvar reached his mind out through Dharanidhar's to his father's. *Bensharie's fine. Tell Rajahansa not to fear. Bensharie is all right. He just wanted to go on an adventure and do something heroic for a change.*

*Heroic like fighting a Great Red dragon? By the fountain, why that?*

Kanvar grimaced. At this distance, the link to his father was too fuzzy to try to explain everything. If Dharanidhar's mind wasn't so ancient and powerful, Kanvar was sure he wouldn't have been able to speak to his father at all. *I'll explain when I get back.*

Kanvar sensed a strange spike in his father's mind, the slightest flit of insinuation that maybe he should not come back. But the connection was so fuzzy he couldn't be sure. Of course he had to go back. Dharanidhar was there if nothing else. Kanvar needed to rejoin his dragon. He thought perhaps he should try to explain to his father about Rajan now instead of waiting, but his father lifted a shield between them and spoke aloud to Dharanidhar.

"Ask Kanvar exactly where he is? What happened in Maran? Was there really another Naga?"

Kanvar heard his father's questions through Dharanidhar's ears and answered. Dharanidhar passed the message back. *They're in the far Eastern Isles at the edge of the world. The Naga from Maran is with them and will no longer be a problem.*

Kanvar hoped that were true. He let his thoughts drift away from Dharanidhar's and looked down at Rajan's pale face. The livid red scar across his cheek would mar him for life, but Kanvar was more worried about the scars inside his mind from the Great Red dragon.

Rajan stirred and looked up at Kanvar with pain-filled eyes. "Who are you? What have you done? We are dead. We are dragon. We are alone." He shuddered violently.

Kanvar bit his lip, pressed his hand against Rajan's head, and forced his body still the way his father had once done to him. He felt dirty for using his power this way, but his intent wasn't to hurt, just to heal. Of course that had been his father's intent too, and Kanvar had hated him for it. Very well, Rajan could hate him, Kanvar would do what Kumar Raza had asked him.

"You are Rajan," Kanvar said, searching through the twisted madness of Rajan's mind for memories of his childhood. He came up against a thick shield, like a steel wall three feet thick. Everything on Kanvar's side of the wall was red dragon bloodthirsty violence. No sign of the memories of the time spent with his brother that Kanvar had witnessed in Kumar Raza's mind.

Kanvar felt along the wall, trying to find a way in, but there were no doors, no windows, no cracks.

Rajan slipped free from Kanvar's mental hold and tried to bite him.

Kanvar jerked back. "Silverwave, can you talk to him? There is a wall in his mind. See if you can get him to take it down."

Silverwave shook her head and slithered away from the boat. She had a strong shield up between her mind and the craziness in Rajan's. Kanvar figured that was probably for the best until he could find some way to free Rajan's early memories.

*Kanvar!*

His grandfather's urgent mental call startled him. He connected with his grandfather's mind. Kumar Raza stood on the cinder cone outside the cave. From his vantage point he could see the water around three-quarters of the island and the wall of Maran warships that were closing in on it.

"Bensharie," Kanvar yelled. "The Maranies are coming. Fly up and get grandfather quickly. Silverwave, pull the boat out into the water. If you can. Are you well enough?"

Silverwave groaned, but grabbed the back of the boat and jerked it out onto the beach and into the waves.

The sudden movement knocked Kanvar off his feet, and he thumped to the bottom of the boat, knocking the lid off the iron pot. Akshara's singing stone howled. Kanvar slammed the lid back on and rubbed his head.

Rajan gasped. "Untie us," he ordered Kanvar using his powers to try to force Kanvar to his will, but he wasn't as strong linked to Silverwave as he had been linked to the Great Red dragon.

Kanvar blocked his command. "I will untie you, I promise. Just as soon as I'm sure you won't eat me."

Bensharie flapped down to them and landed in the water. Kumar Raza climbed off his back into the boat. His armor was still black and rocky. He had a leather satchel slung over his shoulder. "Silverwave, get us out of here. Swim around the island and head straight east."

"East?" Kanvar said in alarm. "East, off the edge of the world?"

"Trust me," Kumar Raza said. "Silverwave, why aren't we moving?"

Silverwave moaned and rolled in the water.

"She's hurt," Kanvar said. "She can't pull us. They were linked when you...killed the red dragon." Kanvar pointed to the horrifying round scar on Rajan's chest. "She has one just like it."

Kumar Raza's face went pale. "Silverwave. I'm sorry."

Silverwave snaked her face up out of the water and licked his cheek.

The Maran flagship rose up from behind the rolling waves. Kanvar's heart froze. Without Silverwave to pull the boat, they were trapped.

Bensharie let out a defiant roar, snatched Silverwave's harness from where it floated on the water, and shot forward, flapping hard. The boat skimmed the waves behind him. Silverwave grabbed onto the side and let it drag her. Her turn to rest.

In a race against the menacing warships, Bensharie got the boat around the island and headed out into open water just before the Maranies hemmed them in.

"Thank the fountain," Kumar Raza said as Bensharie got the life boat far enough away from the Maranies to be safe for the moment. He grabbed his hunting knife and cut Rajan free before Kanvar could stop him.

Hands free. Feet free.

Rajan tackled Kumar Raza and bit his shoulder, almost breaking his teeth against the rock-encrusted armor.

Kumar Raza wrestled Rajan to the bottom of the boat and pinned him down.

"Let me go," Rajan commanded.

Kanvar blocked his mind from forcing Kumar Raza to comply.

"Kanvar, I told you to fix this," Kumar Raza shouted at him.

"I tried," Kanvar said. "There wasn't time. His memories are locked away where I can't reach them. Locked away like your mind was when you hit your head in the Great North." At least Rajan had said *me*. It was the first sign, however small, that he considered himself his own person.

"Well how did you deal with the wall in my mind?"

Rajan arched his back and tried to twist free.

"I...I used a dragonstone to crack the wall. The Great White dragonstone that Denali had. But I don't have it with me now."

"You used a dragonstone?" Kumar Raza looked relieved.

"Yes but—"

"In the satchel. Get it."

Kanvar reached around the struggling men and stuck his hand in the satchel. His fingers rubbed across the smooth facets of a dragonstone, a large one. He tried to pull it out single-handed, but couldn't.

Kumar Raza let go of Rajan with one hand long enough to slip the satchel off of his shoulder and dump the dragonstone out on the bottom of the boat. It was the Great Red dragon's stone, no longer glowing, but colored a sickly blood red that turned Kanvar's stomach.

Kanvar leaned over so his stumpy left hand could help him maneuver the stone over to rest against Rajan's head.

Rajan screamed and tried to break free, but Kumar Raza held him down.

If Kanvar had felt dirty going into Rajan's mind before, it was nothing compared to the pure evil he felt using the red dragon's stone to force his way through Rajan's memories of torment and slam the power of the dragonstone into the steel wall, shattering it.

Rajan's cry of pain as the wall fell nearly tore Kanvar's heart out.

Beyond the wall lay Rajan's childhood, the memories of a warm safe home, and sunny days spent with his twin brother. Happy times. And everything that made him human. But the terror of his years with the red dragon cascaded through the breach in the wall in a flood of pain, self-loathing, and despair, consuming everything that was once bright and good.

Kanvar stood in the breach trying to hold back the flood, but the swirling current swept him off his feet, and he went under. The river of horror stifled his breath and tried to drown him.

*Dharanidhar,* he screamed.

Dharanidhar's mind rushed to surround him. It pulled him to the surface and looked around at the chaos. *What are you trying to do here?*

*Just give me your strength. I have to fix this.* Tying his mind to Dharanidhar's, Kanvar swam through the confusion and grabbed on to one clear memory. Rajan and his brother Kumar hunting. Rajan shot by his uncle, and dying, but Kumar came to his aid. Pulled the crossbow bolt from him and healed the wound with Great dragon saliva. A tender moment, brother to brother.

Then Kanvar gathered the full power of the red dragonstone and turned the monster against itself, slamming every memory after the hunt with his brother into a dark corner at the back of Rajan's mind. Kanvar built a prison there as thick and strong as the wall he'd broken to get in. He trapped every moment with the Great Red dragon behind that wall. Every hurt, every action, every emotion. All of it locked away.

Then he pulled free from Rajan's mind, fell back against the side of the boat, and gasped. His head pounded and his heart beat so fast he thought it might outrun itself. He wiped the memory of the taste of blood and carnage from his mouth and nodded at Grandfather Raza. "He's all yours now."

Rajan had stilled in Kumar Raza's grasp. He blinked and looked up at the giant of a man who held him. "Father?"

Kumar Raza let out a laugh of relief. "No, Rajan. Father's dead. I'm Kumar. Your brother, Kumar. Can't you tell? Here, feel me." He lifted Rajan's hand to his own chest.

Rajan stared into his eyes without saying anything for a long moment. "But Kumar, you're old."

Tears rimmed the edges of Kumar Raza's eyes. "I'm afraid so. We've been separated for a long time."

"No. We've just been hunting together. There was an accident. I...I'm shot." Rajan looked down at his chest. His eyes grew round at the sight of the livid scar. "No crossbow bolt is that big. What is this? What are these other scars?"

Kanvar looked away from mottled, scarred skin from the deep burns that had covered Rajan's chest and arms. He'd felt how Rajan had gotten those when he'd nearly drowned in Rajan's memories.

Kumar Raza lifted his brother up to sit on the bench and handed him a waterskin. "You have been a prisoner of a Great Red volcanic dragon since you and I went hunting in Kundiland. After you were shot, I left you to run get help, but the red dragon captured you while I was gone. I thought you were dead. All this time I thought you were dead. As soon as I found out you were not, I hunted and killed the dragon to free you."

Kanvar noted that Kumar Raza did not mention the fact that their father had also tried to kill Rajan. Kanvar supposed that like the other things, that memory was better forgotten as well.

Rajan finished drinking. "Why can't I remember?"

Kumar Raza accepted the waterskin back from his brother and took a swig himself. "Because it's better that you don't. Your time with the dragon is erased and forgotten. You're starting over now. We both are."

Kanvar winced. He supposed sooner or later he'd have to admit to Grandfather Raza that he had locked up Rajan's memories instead of erasing them. But not now. Not today.

Rajan rubbed his head. "I can feel you, Kumar, but I can feel someone else as well. Something's alive in my head."

Kumar Raza grimaced and raked his fingers through his beard. "Do you remember when you asked Father why we could share each other's thoughts, and he beat you?"

Rajan nodded.

"He did that because our family line descends from a Naga."

"What!"

Kumar Raza lifted a hand. "Let me finish. Father feared that if people knew we could sense each other they would think we were Nagas. The whole family would have been sentenced to death. That is why, when you came down with a fever…remember, you were sick when we went hunting?"

Rajan rubbed his head and shivered. "I felt like I was dying."

"You were. And that is why when you came down with the dragon fever our uncle shot you, to speed you on your way. To end your life before you could bond with a Great dragon." Kumar Raza kicked the dragonstone at his feet so it rolled across the bottom of the boat.

"Is that a Great Red volcanic dragonstone?" Rajan jumped to his feet and tried to grab it, but Kumar Raza caught him and forced him back down.

"Leave it, Rajan."

Kanvar scooped the dragonstone up and wrestled it back into the satchel.

"But it's huge. We'll be rich for life. We will be the most famous dragon hunters that ever lived."

Kanvar laughed.

Rajan frowned at him. "Who are you, and why are you laughing?"

Kanvar choked back his laughter. "I'm your grand-nephew. And that is the third Great Red dragonstone your brother has taken in a hunt. He has already been given the honorific, Raza, the Great Dragon Hunter. No one is more famous than he is."

"My younger brother?" Rajan said in disbelief.

"I'm not younger," Kumar Raza said. "We were born at the same time."

"But I was born first."

"Well I'm older now. Too bad you can't see your face to compare it to mine. You look like you could be my grandson." Kumar Raza ran his fingers through his beard and glanced over at Silverwave submerged in the water beside the boat.

Kanvar cleared his throat. It made him smile to see the brothers banter, but Rajan needed to know the truth about himself. "We were talking about Nagas."

Rajan's face fell, and he was silent for a moment. "Our uncle shot me on purpose?"

"Yes," Kumar Raza said gravely. "Because you had the dragon sickness. Because you are a Naga. The Great Red dragon took you and forced you to bond with it."

Rajan looked over at the bulge in the satchel. "Don't …Nagas…die if their dragon is killed?"

"They do." Kumar Raza leaned over the boat and tapped Silverwave.

The Great Silver serpent lifted her head above the water and snaked it over the side of the boat as Kumar Raza continued speaking. "A Naga will die when his dragon dies, unless he is lucky enough to bond with another Great dragon at the moment his first dragon dies.

Rajan, this is Silverwave. She saved your life, at great risk to her own, to free you from the red dragon. She is the presence you feel in your mind. She is your dragon, and you are her Naga."

Rajan swallowed hard and lifted his hand to rest on Silverwave's dragonstone.

Kanvar shielded his own mind and set to straightening the supplies in the boat. Parmver had taught him that the first few moments when the Naga's and dragon's minds mesh completely were sacred and personal. He motioned for Kumar Raza to leave them alone and let them have their privacy.

Ahead of the boat, Bensharie rippled in golden flight, pulling them over the eastern edge of the world.

## About The Author

**Rebecca Shelley** (Rebecca Lyn Shelley) is the author of over 30 published books including the bestselling **Smart-boys Club** series as well as the popular **Red Dragon Codex** and **Brass Dragon Codex**. She loves writing about dragons and is excited to be writing the **Dragonbound** series. Her **Aos Si** *trilogy* will thrill fans of YA Paranormal Romance. To learn more or contact her, visit her website http://www.rebeccashelley.com.

If you have enjoyed reading **Dragonbound IV: Red Dragon**, Rebecca would love to have you post a review on the site where you purchased it.

# Coming Soon:

**Dragonbound V: Silver Dragon**

Tormented by memories of his time with the Great Red dragon, Rajan struggles to find the humanity within himself and come to terms with the silver dragon he's now bound to. His flight from the Maran warships takes him to the far side of the world where he must face calamity far beyond that of his own troubled past.

**Dragonbound: Dragon Hunter's Guide**

Everything a young dragon hunter needs to know to stay alive, make money, and have fun while hunting dragons.

## Dragonbound V: Silver Dragon Preview
By Rebecca Shelley

# Chapter Three

**"Sailing around the world** in a lifeboat, pulled by a Great Silver serpent, we never dreamed we'd have an adventure like this, eh Kumar?" Rajan knelt at the front of the boat and let the salty breeze slap his face as the boat crested a swell and came down into a trough. "All the boys back home will be so jealous."

Kumar snorted. "All the boys back home who you remember are grown up into old men now. And yes, they're bound to be jealous. I've always outshone them, though I never intended to. Too bad you're a Naga, officially dead, and can't be there when I tell the dragon hunter council about this latest adventure. They probably won't believe me though, no one who ever sailed this far east has returned."

"By the fountain, you're right. How will I ever make my mark as a famous dragon hunter when I'm supposed to be dead? I know, I could take a new identity as your grandson." Rajan spun around to face his brother. Kumar looked old enough to be his grandfather.

"Won't work." Kumar lifted the water skin to his lips, but only a drop trickled out. "The dragon hunter council knows both my grandsons are Nagas. That my daughter married a Naga. They think she killed all three of them herself."

"Maybe you had another child." Rajan scrabbled to find some sense of identity he could present to the world.

"I did, and he's a Naga. Young though. Only twelve. He hasn't come down with the fever yet." Kumar smiled wistfully. "He's a good boy."

Rajan leaned forward. "So? I could still be your son. Older. Born before him."

Kumar dropped the empty water skin. "Rajan. You *cannot* go to Daro. They will recognize you, and they will kill you."

Kumar's words felt like he had struck Rajan in the face. He winced. "But…how could they, if I've been locked up in the red dragon's lair all these years?" He felt around in his mind, trying to find the memories that would confirm he'd been with the red dragon. He came up against a wall, thick, smooth, and blank.

Kumar growled under his breath. "Our water's gone. The food is gone. Ask Silverwave if she can tell how close we are to those islands."

"Who cares about food and water? Don't change the subject. You're hiding something from me, and I want to know what it is. Why can't I go to Daro? How could they possibly recognize me?" Rajan dug his nails into the wooden bench he sat on and wondered for a flash second why his claws could not tear the bench to splinters. He jerked his hands away. His eyes stung as he stared at his brother, but Kumar set his jaw and said nothing.

A feral growl sprang unbidden from Rajan's throat. He tried to spread his wings, leap across the boat, and sink his teeth into his brother's neck. But his leap only took him a quarter of the way, and he landed flat on his stomach. The impact forced the air out of his lungs. He gasped but couldn't draw more in. Sliding off the bench, he curled into a ball on the floor of the boat.

"Rajan." Kumar knelt beside him and rubbed his back, forcing his lungs to open up and accept air. "Come on. Breathe."

Rajan managed to suck in enough air to moan. His mind spun from burning magma to cool ocean depths.

*Stay here with me,* Silverwave whispered into his mind. *We are cool water. We are peace.*

Rajan gritted his teeth, pulled away from his brother, and slipped over the side of the boat to join Silverwave. She caught him as he went under, and he wrapped his arms around her torso, letting her pull him to the surface where they skimmed along as she hauled the boat with his brother in it behind them.

Hours later an island came into view on the horizon. Rajan was chilled numb from the cold ocean, but he didn't want to get back into the boat with Kumar. He stayed with Silverwave until she crawled out of the water onto the rocky beach. A forest of pine trees covered mountain slopes above the water. A blast of cold air battered Rajan's face. He tried to walk, but his legs were too numb to carry him.

Kumar jumped out of the boat as soon as Silverwave drew it up onto the shore. He pulled Rajan's arm up over his shoulders and helped him stumbled away from the water into the trees. Neither of them said anything to each other as Kumar gathered wood and started a fire.

"Silverwave," Kumar called to the serpent who had coiled herself on the beach. "See if you can find a stream inlet along the coast close to here. We need fresh water."

Silverwave uncurled and returned to the water.

Rajan tried to get up to follow her, but Kumar restrained him with a strong hand on his shoulder. "Stay by the fire. You're wet and you're cold. You'll get hypothermia if you don't dry off and warm up." He checked the crossbow and bolts on his back. "I'm going to hunt us some dinner. Keep the fire going."

As Kumar strode away, Rajan edged closer to the fire and put his palms up to warm them. The sun was setting, and the forest would soon be dark. He strained to hear the sounds of the animals that must be lurking in the trees. He'd memorized which lesser dragons thrived in different habitats around the world, which ones on which continents, but this was a new place. Not so different really than the northern pine forests of Kundiland, right? He heard the chatter of squirrels, the chirp of birds. He listened more closely for the rasp of lesser brown raptor scales against tree bark. Though the raptors were only knee high, they hunted in packs and moved in silence through a forest. Only the rustle of leaves of the faint sound of their scales rubbing against the trees would give away their location. He glanced at the tree trunks around him and the branches overhead. They would come from all sides and from above. Their scales looked like tree bark. They could hold still on a trunk for hours waiting for their prey.

He saw no sign of the raptors, heard no sound that would forewarn an attack. "Be the hunter or be hunted," he reminded himself the lesson his instructors had drilled into his head. What else might be on this island? Black dragons or green dragons of various varieties, serpents in the streams and lakes.

A twig snapped behind him.

He drew his sword and jumped to his feet. He had no armor, only a flimsy linen shirt and trousers.

*What do we have here?* A thought swelled in his mind. *Smells human.*

A mottled gray and black shadow moved beyond the trees a dozen yards away. A Great dragon of some kind, since Rajan had heard its thoughts, not just impressions from its mind.

*I'm not human.* Rajan set his stance, in case the dragon attacked him. It was so well camouflaged he could not yet be sure of its shape and size.

A sharp hiss rattled the trees. It was big then, big enough Rajan wished he had Kumar's crossbow.

*A Naga? It has been long since a Naga has flown to these shores. But I do not smell a gold dragon with you.* The words rumbled through his mind, deep and ancient. He sensed the dragon now. It was big, but seldom moved far, content to let the forest creatures wander into range of its jaws to be snapped up in an instant.

*I'm bound to a silver serpent,* Rajan said.

*Impossible.*

*No, or I wouldn't be bound to her.*

*I thought the Nagas were extinct.*

*So did I.*

A shadow moved near the closest tree beside Rajan.

Rajan shifted to face it, sword raised.

Kumar stepped out, motioning for Rajan to be silent. He pointed into the shadows where the Great dragon lay and lifted his crossbow to take aim.

"No." Rajan leaped forward and grabbed the crossbow from his hands. "He's a Great dragon. Leave him alone."

Kumar shrugged. "Probably too big to eat anyway, but are you sure it's friendly?"

*Are you friend or foe?* Rajan asked the dragon.

A rumble of laugher like rocks rolling down a hill filled the forest. *The Naga asks if I am a friend. I would ask the same of it, but I know it is not. I tell you, I will die before I return to slavery at your hands.*

"Slavery? I would not. Could not. What?" Rajan said aloud. He shoved Kumar's crossbow back into his hands and readied his sword.

*So you say.* Trees creaked and pine needles rustled as the old dragon got to its feet. It was huge. Dirt and plants that had grown on its back during its long years of immobility cascaded to the ground.

"We mean you no harm. We want nothing from you!" Rajan shouted. "Leave us alone, and we'll leave you alone."

The dragon spread its wings above the trees, and mottled black scales glinted in the setting sun. Its head snaked up as it bared its teeth.

"Do you suppose it breathes fire?" Rajan whispered to Kumar.

"Great Black forest dragon. Probably not. Can't you convince it we're not enemies?"

"You heard me try. It didn't work."

"You're a Naga, convince him."

"I'm a Naga. That's the problem. He—"

A spray of burning black goo shot from the dragon's throat. Rajan dove to one side, Kumar to the other. Rajan rolled to his feet and dodged behind a tree.

Kumar got a shot off with the crossbow that hit the dragon in its throat. "That ought to keep him from spraying tar for a moment."

The dragon let out a gurgling roar of pain and swatted at Kumar and Rajan with his heavy tail, knocking a row of trees over in the process. Rajan dropped to the ground, so the tail passed over top of him. Kumar jumped onto the tale as it swung past and ran up it onto the dragon's back.

"Make it stop, Rajan!" Kumar yelled. "I don't want to have to kill it." He aimed his second bolt at the dragon's eye as it twisted its head around to tear him off its back.

*Stop. Please stop!* Rajan spoke into the angry dragon's mind. *We're friends. I have not come to enslave you. I would never do that to anyone.*

*Liar!*

The dragon snapped its jaws toward Kumar. Kumar's finger moved on the trigger.

*"Stop! Both of you!"* Rajan shouted putting all his will and mental energy behind the command.

Both dragon and dragon hunter froze in place, a split second away from killing each other.

The rush of power made Rajan giddy. He sucked in a heated breath, realizing that he could control anyone, make them do anything. No one could stop him. He could make all the world bow to his commands. The dragon and his brother remained frozen in place. Neither could move without his permission. Neither could speak. The forest went dead still. For several long moments nothing moved.

*I can't breathe. Let me breathe*, the dragon's thoughts came as a desperate whisper into his mind. Rajan realized with horror that neither the dragon nor Kumar could breathe. He had stopped them completely. He could just as easily have stopped their hearts.

*"Breathe!"* he shouted. But his own breath caught in his throat. He could have killed them. Accidentally, with a single command. *"Neither of you will hurt each other from now on,"* he said. Then he left them and ran, back to the beach,

back to the water, calling for Silverwave, frightened of himself, horrified by what he'd become.

He shivered as the chill evening air cut through his wet clothes. Silverwave was up the coast. It would take her a few minutes to reach him. He sheathed his sword, wrapped his arms around himself, and started walking, his teeth chattering. The round stones of the beach made his steps awkward and uneven. The ocean surf hissed and sprayed.

I'm a Naga, he thought. Power, so much power. Corrupts. I should be dead. What have I become. I cannot live with this. *Oh please, Silverwave, help me. I'm so cold. So lost.* He wished for Daro's sunshine and desert sand. For the happy chatter of shoppers in the street, the clucking of itchekins and the mewl of kitrats. He had a pet kitrat once, Little Ravi, cuddly scales and a tail that used to wrap clear around his arm when he carried him out of the house. I want to go home. I don't want to be a Naga. I'm a dragon hunter. I live in Daro. I have a twin brother my same age. This is all a dream, a nightmare. He splashed into a tide pool, twisted his ankle, and fell to his knees.

Strong arms lifted from the pool and embraced him. His brother's arms, grown so much bigger and older than him. "It's all right, Rajan. Come back to the fire. You're freezing. No harm done. The dragon has settled back to sleep."

"No harm? How can you say that? I nearly killed you. Both of you. And…and… and just for a moment I thought I enjoyed it. I wanted to use my power. To control people. To hurt people. Kumar, please, just kill me now. I'm a monster. You can't trust me. I can't trust myself. There's something evil inside me. I can feel it." Rajan couldn't stop shaking. The cold wind seemed to wrap around his heart and freeze it.

"There was evil in you," Kumar's deep voice rumbled. "But I purged it. I killed the red dragon. It can no longer control you. No longer make you do things against your will."

Rajan shuddered. "I don't know what has happened. You've hidden it from me. I don't know what I've done. But what if I didn't do anything against my will? What if I wanted to be bound to the red dragon?" Pain of betrayal and hunger for revenge spread like ice crystals from his frozen heart. "You can't change the person I am inside. You can't make me a better man, just by changing what dragon I'm bound to."

"You're cold. Hypothermic. Talking nonsense. Now come with me back to the fire. We'll get you out of those wet clothes, wrap you up in a blanket, get some warm food in you, and you'll be fine. You'll get some rest, and tomorrow will be a better day." Kumar Raza forced Rajan back into the trees and over to the fire.

Rajan went along without further protest, but inside he doubted he'd be any better in the morning."

www.ingramcontent.com/pod-product-compliance
Lightning Source LLC
Chambersburg PA
CBHW070819180626
46818CB00001B/331

# PILGRIM TALES

## A Catholic Writers Guild
## Short Story Anthology

Nancy Bechel
Isabelle Wood
Karen Meyer
Karina Fabian
John Ruberto
Laura Ruberto
Corinna Turner
Rietta Parker
Judy D'Ammasso Tarbox
A.R.K. Watson
Mary McWilliams
Andrew Seddon
Jane Lebak
Mary Jo Thayer
G. M. Baker

Catholic
**Writers Guild**

INDIANAPOLIS, INDIANA

**Catholic Writers Guild**
**Indianapolis, IN**
**https://catholicwritersguild.com**

Publisher's Note: These are works of fiction. Names, characters, places, and incidents are a product of the author's imagination. Locales and public names are sometimes used for atmospheric purposes. Any resemblance to actual people, living or dead, or to businesses, companies, events, institutions, or locales is completely coincidental.

Book Layout © 2017 BookDesignTemplates.com
Cover art by Kelsey Gietl
  ➢ "The Arrival in Bethlehem" comes from the Metropolitan Museum of Art, NY, Open Access Collection

**Pilgrim Tales/ Various Authors.**—1st ed.
Print ISBN: 979-8-9939351-0-2